P.oW

Martin Booth

PUFFIN BOOKS

PUFFIN BOOKS

Published by the Penguin Group

Penguin Books Ltd, 27 Wrights Lane, London W8 5TZ, England

Penguin Putnam Inc., 375 Hudson Street, New York, New York 10014, USA

Penguin Books Australia Ltd, Ringwood, Victoria, Australia

Penguin Books Canada Ltd, 10 Alcorn Avenue, Toronto, Ontario, Canada M4V 3B2

Penguin Books (NZ) Ltd, Private Bag 102902, NSMC, Auckland, New Zealand

On the World Wide Web at: www.penguin.com

Penguin Books Ltd, Registered Offices: Harmondsworth, Middlesex, England

First published 2000

1 3 5 7 9 10 8 6 4 2

The moral right of the author has been asserted

Set in Bembo

Made and printed in England by Clays Ltd, St Ives plc

British Library Cataloguing in Publication Data

A CIP catalogue record for this book is available from the British Library

ISBN 0–141–30421–9

This story is dedicated to the memory of my grandfather, Chief Petty Officer George Pankhurst, who was cast into the sea when his destroyer, HMS *Nomad*, was sunk by enemy fire at the Battle of Jutland, at approximately five o'clock on the afternoon of 31 May 1916.

A glossary of naval and other terms used in the book can be found at the end.

PART ONE

MAY 1916

Ted leaned forward and peered dubiously into the bowl placed before him on the table. It contained a thick and glutinous soup with nondescript lumps of what might once have been fatty meat floating just below the surface. On the rim of the bowl was perched a ship's biscuit as square as a floor tile and about as thick. He prodded a piece of the suspect meat with his spoon and was about to scoop it up and eat it when there was a tiny splash near the edge of the bowl.

He glanced around. Everyone on the mess-deck was either slurping down his own bowl of soup or busy softening his biscuit in it.

Plot!

Something else landed in his soup. Ted looked up. The ceiling over his head was shiny with water, small drops of which were falling into his soup from the head of a rivet in the steel plating of the deck above.

'Condensation, shipmate,' commented the sailor sitting next to him.

'Condensation?' Ted echoed.

'That's right,' replied the sailor. 'See, it's warm in 'ere

but outside, it's cold. So, what with the steam off the soup an' the breath of all us jack tars … Well, it stands to reason, don't it?'

'Does it?' Ted asked.

'Course it do,' was the answer. 'Warm one side, cold t'other. Condensation.'

Ted nodded: then it dawned on him. The drops of water falling into his soup had been, before they had collected on the rivet, the invisible steam of men's breath. He put his spoon down, his appetite gone.

'Don't you want your soup?' enquired a sailor sitting opposite him.

Ted shook his head. Those drops, he considered, might just as well be tiny gobs of spit. He slid his bowl over the table.

'Ta!' exclaimed the sailor gratefully as he snapped Ted's biscuit in two and pushed it under the surface of the soup with his spoon. 'Ta very muchly.'

Taking a hunk of bread from a loaf at the end of the table, Ted left the mess-deck and, climbing the steep companionway to the deck above, found himself near the stern of the ship. A stiff, cold wind was blowing in off the Solent but he paid it no heed. Hoisting himself up on to the platform of a deck-mounted gun, he bit off a piece of the dry bread and, staring miserably at the sea, started to chew upon it. If, he thought self-pityingly, he froze to death, it would be a blessing in disguise.

'You all right, son?'

Ted turned. Behind him stood one of the sailors from the mess-deck. He was wearing what Ted knew were called Number 8s, dark-blue trousers with a dark-blue shirt over which hung the square blue collar edged with white of a naval rating. Round his neck was his black silk and a lanyard. Upon his left sleeve was embroidered a dark-red anchor under which was a single chevron while, on his right, there were two crossed flags with a small diamond above and below them.

'I saw you leave the mess,' the sailor continued. 'This your first ship?'

'Yes, sir,' Ted admitted somewhat glumly.

'And you came here straight from HMS *Ganges*?'

'Yes, sir,' Ted repeated.

'Then you've been up the mast.'

Ted nodded. Everyone at HMS *Ganges*, the training school, had had to go up the mast. It was part of the training to climb what had once been the foremast of a famous sailing ship, a man-o'-war called HMS *Elephant*.

'Been up it myself,' the sailor continued, sitting on the gun platform next to Ted, 'when I first joined the Navy. Scared me half out of my wits.'

'Me too,' Ted admitted. He clearly recalled his terror, clinging to a rope on the third spar up the mast, his knuckles white and his mind swimming with fear.

'How far did you climb?'

'Third fighting top, sir,' Ted replied.

'Well, that's better than I did,' the sailor said. 'I only made it to the second. My name's George Pankhurst,' he introduced himself. 'I'm the Leading Signalman on board. And I'm the Leading Hand of your mess-deck. Bit homesick, are you?'

Ted hesitated and lowered his head, unwilling to

admit it. He was in a man's world now and he did not want to let himself down.

'No need to be ashamed, lad,' Pankhurst said comfortingly. 'We're all a bit off our sorts on a new ship. There isn't one man below who isn't thinking of his loved ones this very minute.' He looked at the sea. As the evening drew on, it was darkening to the colour of polished jet. At the entrance to the harbour, a lighthouse flashed intermittently. Along the shore, dim lights began to show in buildings. 'What's your name?'

'Ted Foley, sir,' Ted said.

'And how old are you?'

Just for a split second, Ted hesitated again before declaring, as firmly as he could, 'Fifteen, sir.'

For a moment, Pankhurst stared hard at him. Ted felt his cheeks start to warm and colour with a guilty blush. It was not the truth. He was fourteen and had lied when standing before the recruiting officer in Plymouth. Yet no one had questioned him. The Great War had been going on for well over a year and the Royal Navy needed sailors, be they ship's boys or officer cadets. Now here he was, on board a warship in Portsmouth harbour, with the future stretching endlessly and uncertainly ahead of him. Not for the first time, he wondered if he had done the right thing.

'Well, Ted Foley,' Pankhurst said, breaking into a smile, 'welcome to HMS *Nomad*. I hope she'll be a happy berth for you.'

'Thank you, sir,' Ted replied.

Pankhurst chuckled and said, 'I'm not sir. You

address the officers as Sir, the Chief Petty Officer as Chief and the Petty Officer as PO, but you call me Leading Hand. Now then, Ted,' he went on, 'what do you know about *Nomad*?'

'She's a destroyer,' Ted said. That much he had been told by the dispatcher when he received his orders and travel warrant on leaving *Ganges*.

'She's an M-class destroyer,' Pankhurst corrected him. 'Brand, spanking new, launched just three months ago. Not a chip of rust or a loose bolt to be found on her. Armed with –' he jerked his thumb over his shoulder at the weapon on the platform behind them – 'three 4-inch QF Mark IV guns, one for'ard, one aft and one amidships, a pom-pom and four torpedo tubes. And she has a complement of eighty men, including four officers.'

From across the water echoed the distant whistle of a train. It was a sad, lonesome sound and it momentarily made Ted feel even more miserable. He sensed tears welling into his eyes and fought to drive them back.

'*Nomad*'s in the thirteenth Flotilla,' Pankhurst went on, pretending not to notice Ted's misery. 'We're to be attached to the Battlecruiser Fleet and the 5th Battle Squadron.' He paused. 'Look over there.'

Ted squinted into the twilight.

'Isn't that a sight to set your heart pounding?' Pankhurst asked.

Somewhat puzzled by the question, Ted replied, 'Yes, sir,' then quickly corrected himself. 'Yes, Leading Hand.'

Silhouetted against the encroaching night was a forest of masts and funnels, rigging and, behind them, squat military warehouses.

'That's the greatest navy the world has ever known,' Pankhurst said. 'Rodney, Hood, Horatio Nelson: they all looked upon this view the day before they sailed. Just like you and me. You'll never feel more proud of yourself than you do now, knowing that you're a part of it. For as long as you're a man, even after you leave the Navy, you'll still always be a British sailor.'

As if in agreement with Pankhurst, a signal lamp on the bridge of a warship alongside a quay started to flash. It might, Ted thought, have been a bright star twinkling low down in the deepening night and, as he watched it, he felt that pride beginning to stir in him, to start to eat away at his self-doubt and unhappiness.

'Why don't you come on down to the mess-deck now?' Pankhurst suggested. 'It's getting a bit parky out here.'

Tossing his uneaten piece of bread into the sea, Ted followed Pankhurst below. On the mess-deck, the meal had been cleared away and the sailors were relaxing. Seated at one table, four played cards, snapping them down on the scrubbed deal surface. Beside them, another was writing a letter, shielding it from the others' view like a schoolboy preventing someone from copying his answers. At another an elderly seaman, his ditty box open by his side, was sewing up a tear in a shirt.

'You get your head down,' Pankhurst advised. 'Tomorrow's going to be a busy day.' He turned to the letter-writer and said, 'Sharkey, this is Ted Foley. Help him to sling his hammock.'

'Yes, Leading Hand,' Sharkey replied, folding his letter over so no one could read it. 'Let's see to you then, lad.'

6

Half an hour later, Ted lay in his hammock, suspended from two hooks mounted into the iron bulkhead on either side of the mess-deck. Several other sailors had also turned in, one of them starting to snore gently. Below, at a table, Sharkey was finishing off his letter by the glow of a dim light. The air was warm and close and, Ted thought, strangely homely. It reminded him of his mother's kitchen, with the hammocks hanging like clothes suspended from the drying frame above the stove.

As he drifted off to sleep, Ted thought of his home in the North Devon village of Clovelly: the steep valley sides upon which the houses stood, the terraced gardens and the church with its ancient tombs, the cobbled street too steep for a horse and cart up which his Uncle Arthur drove his donkeys, and the little harbour beneath with its huddle of boats. One of these was the *Evelyn*, the single-masted skiff in which he had so often helped his father trawl for sardines or sail round their crab pots out in Bideford Bay. He could hear the sea washing on the shingle and the calls of the fishermen as they readied their boats for a day's fishing or a journey taking trippers out to Lundy Island. The village seemed so far away. He tried to picture his mother's face and found, to his dismay, that he could not quite conjure it up.

The following morning, Ted was given a tour of HMS *Nomad* by Pankhurst.

Less than eighty-five metres long, *Nomad* had three

7

funnels, a mainmast just aft of the bridge and a smaller, radio communications mast two-thirds of the way back. At the base of the radio mast was the pom-pom gun while astern of it was a powerful searchlight. The bridge was barely five metres above the main deck which, in turn, was little more than three metres from the surface of the sea. The entire vessel was painted grey except for a white identification letter and number on the side of the hull and the brass fittings, every one of which shone with polishing.

On the bridge, they came upon the Captain, Lt Cmdr Whitfield, poring over a set of navigation charts for the North Sea. Ted came to attention and saluted.

'New ship's boy, sir,' Pankhurst announced. 'Junior Seaman Foley, sir.'

'Very smart,' Whitfield said, acknowledging the salute. 'Good to have you with us, Foley.'

'His first ship, sir,' Pankhurst went on.

'Is it, indeed,' the officer remarked, looking Ted straight in the eye. 'Your first ship's very important. This is where you start your career in the Royal Navy. You'll serve on many ships but you'll never forget your first. Make sure you do right by her and she'll do right by you. Carry on.'

The last place they visited was the engine room. It was cramped and claustrophobic, with three huge oil-fired boilers providing steam for the electricity generators and turbine-driven ship's engines. Even though *Nomad* was not under way, it was noisy and hot in the confined space. Every surface, pipe and valve seemed to radiate heat. Ted was glad when they returned to the fresh air of the deck.

'So what do you think of her?' Pankhurst asked as they stepped out on deck.

'She's ...' Ted was not quite sure how to put it '... not very big.'

'No,' said Pankhurst, 'but her size is her strength. Those turbines can drive her at thirty-four knots, even through a heavy sea. She can turn on a sixpence. If the Captain orders hard over, and the engines are at full speed, she'll lean over like a clipper going about in a hurricane. You'll need to hang on, you mark my words.'

A tender was moored alongside. Sailors were unloading boxes from her and carrying them below. Ted and Pankhurst stepped aside to avoid getting in their way.

'It's the destroyer's job to harry the enemy,' Pankhurst explained. 'Surprise him. Catch him off his guard. Our guns aren't our main weapons. Compared to the 15-inch guns on battleships, our 4-inch guns are little more than pea-shooters. Our primary weapons are these.' Pankhurst stopped and placed his hand on a round metal casing about six metres long with the girth of a large barrel. 'Do you know what this is?'

Ted did. 'Torpedo tubes, Leading Hand,' he said.

'That's right. You can hit a ship over and over again with gunfire and she'll still float, still hold her course. Yet one of these, exploding just below the water line ...' Pankhurst snapped his fingers and left the rest of his sentence unspoken.

Leading Ted down a passageway beneath the bridge, Pankhurst stopped outside a door and knocked. A gruff voice told them to enter. When the door opened, the first thing Ted noticed was the strong aroma of pipe tobacco mixed with the scents of paper and leather wafting out of the cabin.

'Ship's boy, Chief,' Pankhurst said.

Seated at a desk, surrounded by shelves of ledgers, books and files, was Chief Petty Officer Crane. His face, where it showed through a full, dark beard, was tanned by years of stiff sea breezes. His eyes were slightly narrowed by just as many years peering into the vastness of the ocean.

On the bulkhead above his desk, a brass-cased maritime chronometer clicked loudly. Next to it, his cap hung from a hook below which, in a dainty silver frame that looked most out of place in such a masculine setting, was a sepia photograph of a young couple on their wedding day. Through the porthole came the sound of the tender casting off, its fenders grinding along *Nomad*'s hull.

'Morning, boy,' he greeted Ted, swivelling round in his chair.

'Good morning, Chief,' Ted replied, remembering Pankhurst's instruction. He also remembered not to salute. You never saluted a superior unless he was wearing his cap and could return the salutation.

'That'll be all, George,' the Chief said to Pankhurst. 'Carry on.'

Pankhurst left the cabin, closing the door quietly behind him.

'So, what have we here?' the Chief mused aloud, looking Ted up and down. 'A young whipper-snapper setting off on his long journey across the seven seas. A boy ready to be a man. Are you ready to be a man, boy?'

'Yes, Chief,' Ted answered, a little nervously. He had not considered such a question before and wondered now if he really was ready.

'Excellent! But remember this: you're not just any man. You're a sailor and a sailor in His Majesty's Royal Navy. You've got centuries of tradition behind you. Brave men before you to live up to. Never let them down. Set an example for boys in the future to follow. Boys like you. Here –' he turned to his desk – 'what's this?'

He held out a length of cord with a complicated knot in it. Ted took it and turned it over in his hands.

'It's a bowline, Chief.'

For a moment, he thought he was wrong. The Chief looked hard at Ted as if searching his soul for any weakness he might exploit. One of his eyebrows rose a centimetre. Ted studied the knot again.

'On the bight,' Ted added.

The Chief took the cord back. His hands moved as quickly as a skilful magician's as he undid the knot and tied another.

'And this one, lad?' he asked, holding the cord out again.

Ted had no need to take it. He had seen his father tie that knot many a time on the deck of the *Evelyn*.

'It's a Carrick Bend, Chief.'

'Well done, lad!' the Chief exclaimed. He tossed the cord on to a shelf. 'Now, let's sort out your duties. A ship's boy is a dogsbody but that doesn't mean you'll be slave to every matelot aboard. You have set tasks to perform every day. You will serve at table in the officers' mess, share the various deck chores of your comrades and be available when a spare hand is needed. Show willing at all times, watch and listen. As a dogsbody, you'll learn a lot which'll stand you in good stead for the rest of your life. Any questions?'

As the Chief was speaking, one thought had been foremost in Ted's mind. This was a warship and Britain was at war with the Kaiser's Germany. It was inevitable that *Nomad* would go into action and that that would happen sooner rather than later. When she did, Ted wondered, what would his role be then? Yet he was worried about asking. Perhaps, he considered, it was not his place to speak up.

'I know what's on your mind,' the Chief said, cutting into Ted's silence. 'Don't you worry, you'll have a part to play when the time comes. And you'll start learning it this afternoon. You're a member of the Number 3 gun crew. You know which gun that is?'

'The one at the stern, Chief.'

'Spot on!' the Chief retorted. 'You report to Mr Bellingham, the Gunner, at 14:00 hours. As for now, report to AB Catchpole in the galley. He's the officers' steward. Off you go. And,' he added as Ted reached for the cabin door, 'don't be afraid to ask questions. Asking is learning.'

Ted spent the remainder of the morning in the officers' wardroom, where he was taught by the mess steward how to lay a table, align the cutlery, fold the napkins and position the glasses. This done, he was shown how to serve food, always standing to the left of the seated officer, holding the serving dish or bowl in both hands but with, as Catchpole put it, 'None of yer fingers inboard.'

At one o'clock, he was given the first opportunity to put the lessons into practice. Kitted out in a starched white jacket, his hair neatly combed and his boots polished like ebony, Ted stood to one side, watching as Catchpole served the ship's officers with grilled pork chops. He followed with boiled potatoes as the steward served peas and sliced carrots. Finally, Ted went round the table with the gravy tureen.

As they ate, Ted studied the officers. The Captain apart, it was his first encounter with them. Lt Haliley, the second-in-command, was talkative and he, the Captain and Lt Cmdr Benoy, the Chief Engineer, had a long but amicable argument about the tactics to be employed with submarines. *Nomad*, Ted discovered, had an especially strengthened bow to enable it to ram submarines at speed. The fourth officer was a young Sub-Lieutenant called Wainwright whom the others addressed as Subby. He was quiet and ate his food without trying to take part in the conversation, only speaking when spoken to.

At precisely 14:00 hours, as four bells sounded from the bridge, Ted presented himself to Bellingham. He was a taciturn man who seemed to have something on his mind. Ted found out what it was as he marched behind the Gunner towards the stern.

'You listen here, Junior Seaman,' Bellingham said with a chilling formality, spitting out Ted's rank as if it was a foul taste in his mouth. 'I'm not in favour of having a ship's boy in a gun crew. It's a job for a man and a dependable one, at that.' He stopped in his tracks and turned. 'One mistake from you and not only your comrades are placed in danger but so is the whole ship.

You make one cock-up, boy,' he almost snarled, 'and I'll wear your guts for gaiters. Got that?'

'Yes, sir,' Ted replied timorously.

'Sir?' Bellingham snorted.

'Leading Hand?' Ted ventured.

'I'm not … God preserve us from dolts and dunderheads. I'm the Gunner! Got it?'

'Yes, Gunner,' Ted said.

They reached Number 3 gun. Two sailors were busy greasing the gearing of the mounting. One of them was Sharkey.

'You!' Bellingham exclaimed. 'Show this little piece of snot the ropes.'

When the Gunner had left them, Sharkey said, 'Don't you worry about him. He's a good man but he gets wound up, like. Feels the responsibility.' He swung himself on to the gun platform. 'Jump up on here.'

For twenty minutes, Sharkey introduced Ted to every part of the gun. By the end, his head was filled with words he did not understand – actuating plunger, buffer block, pawl and firing spindle.

'Feeling punch drunk?' Sharkey asked as he ended his lecture. 'No need to be. See, this gun has a seven-man crew. And you're the Ammunition Number. The seventh man. You don't have to operate the gun. Your job's to provide the ordnance. See …' He pulled a small buff-coloured book from his pocket and opened it to show a diagram of the gun. 'It goes like this. The shell comes up from the magazine below decks on a hoist.' He pointed to the diagram then a small hatchway forward of the gun platform. 'You take it and hand it to the Loader. That's me. I set the fuse on the shell

14

according to what the Sightsetters tell me – they're the ones that aim the gun – and pass it to the Breech Loader. He inserts it into the breech and closes the breech block. That,' he put his hand on the rear of the barrel, 'is this bit that looks like a small door. When everything's set, the Trainer points the gun, the Gunlayer fires the gun by pulling on a cord that is attached to the firing lever and Bob's your uncle! Simplicity itself. Just like the works of a wheelbarrow.' He looked up at the funnels. Smoke was beginning to drift away on the breeze. 'You'll soon get the hang of it. We're putting to sea in half an hour. The gun sights've got to be calibrated and everything made shipshape.'

As *Nomad* sailed to the gunnery range, the Number 3 gun crew trained hard. At first, Ted was clumsy and slowed them up but no one cursed at or criticized him and, after an hour, he moved with the rhythm of the other men, learning to predict the next command, the next action in the chain of events that started with his leaning into the hatch for a dummy practice shell and ended with the almost inaudible click of the firing pin.

The shells with their brass casings were heavy. By the time they reached the artillery range twelve nautical miles off The Needles, the most westerly point of the Isle of Wight, his back ached, his arms felt as if they had been torn from his shoulders and his fingers were numb with the cold. His lips tasted of sea salt and his hands smelt of brass and lubricating oil.

At five o'clock, *Nomad* turned to sail at a steady ten knots through a light swell. A nautical mile to starboard, a tug kept abreast of her, towing what looked, to Ted, like a massive garden trellis covered with canvas. Sharkey explained it was a gunnery target. When, finally, it was time to go into action, Ted was exhausted.

'You ready?' Sharkey asked as they stood at their stations.

Ted nodded but he was unsure of himself. He knew what his role was but he wondered if he had the strength left to carry it out.

Sharkey reached into his pocket and pulled out a small roll of lint bandage. 'Nearly forgot,' he added, tearing off two thin strips. 'Roll these up and stuff them in your ears,' he ordered Ted. 'It's noisy work we do.'

'Number 3 gun,' Bellingham yelled through a loudhailer, 'commence firing.'

As the order was given, Ted suddenly found his heart pounding with excitement and he discovered a new reserve of strength. Almost without thinking, he went through the motions, checking the hoist, taking the shell out of its cradle and handing it to Sharkey. When the gun fired, he felt a surge of power run through him like an electric charge. Despite the stuffing, his head rang with the explosion.

The first practice shell fell well short, making a small, almost indiscernible splash as it hit the sea. A signal lamp on the bridge of the tug flashed the degree of error. The second passed over the target and the third hit the sea just ahead of it. The fourth struck the canvas sheeting, ripping a hole in it. Even from a mile off, the rent was obvious and the gun crew cheered. Bellingham ordered them to stand down.

As the gun crew made good, lightly greasing any

moving parts against the sea spray, polishing any tarnished brass, replacing the canvas cover over the gun and putting the spent cartridge cases, still warm from the firing, in a tray for taking below, Sharkey turned to Ted and said, 'Well done, lad. We'll make a powder monkey out of you yet.'

'A powder monkey?' Ted responded, a little annoyed at being compared to such an animal.

'That's right. You know what a powder monkey was, don't you?' Sharkey did not wait for Ted to reply. 'In the days of sailing ships, the powder monkey was a young lad, often a good few years younger than you are, nimble and quick of foot, whose job it was to run from the gunpowder locker to the cannon, carrying the explosive charges. A highly responsible job. If he slipped on the deck …' He put his hands together as if in prayer and briefly cast his eyes upwards.

As *Nomad* sailed back in the gathering twilight towards Portsmouth, Ted stood by the stern and watched the ship's wake boiling away behind her. For the first time since he had marched in through the gates of the training school, he felt he was, at least in part, a real sailor.

Four days later, *Nomad*, with three other destroyers, put to sea. In fine, spring sunshine, they steamed along the English Channel, keeping fairly close in to the British shore. Passing the White Cliffs of Dover, they altered course and, after clearing Ramsgate, made full speed ahead across the Thames estuary. Reaching Harwich at dusk, they hove to and anchored in the mouth of the River Orwell.

The mood on the mess-deck that night was subdued. No shore leave was permitted and the crew were edgy. They were now in the North Sea, within easy range of German submarines and in waters where the Germans were surreptitiously laying mines. As soon as darkness fell, no lights were shown at all. Every watch was doubled and no one was spared duty. To a casual observer, *Nomad* might have been a ghost ship or just a darker patch of night set against the shore.

Just before midnight, Ted was roused from a deep and dreamless sleep by Pankhurst gently rocking his hammock.

'Look sharp! Time to do your turn on watch,' he whispered.

Ted swung out of his hammock and, within five minutes, found himself next to Sharkey on the very prow of *Nomad*, staring out into the night. The estuary to the Orwell was familiar to both of them: HMS *Ganges* was only a short distance up-river and it was here both Ted and Sharkey had sailed dinghies during their training. Yet neither of them spoke, or even allowed their memories to interrupt their thoughts. They needed clear heads and sharp minds to penetrate the night for hidden danger.

By four o'clock, when the watch changed, Ted's eyes were tired and stinging. He returned to his hammock and, although he closed his smarting eyes, he could not sleep. The concentration required to watch for a stealthy periscope cutting through the waves had made his nerves so taut he could not relax. When, an hour later, *Nomad* got up steam, slipped her anchor and, second in the line, headed out to sea in convoy with the other destroyers, he got up and watched Harwich disappear astern.

For most of the morning, Ted turned his hand to general chores about the ship until, at noon, he was back on duty, this time on the bridge where he was told to be available if needed and to keep his eyes peeled. Pankhurst stood near him, observing the destroyer steaming ahead of them.

Ted had been on watch for about an hour when a signal lamp starting blinking on the destroyer leading their little convoy.

'Signal from *Moorsom*, sir,' Pankhurst announced, translating it as it came to him. '"Drifting … mine … sighted … off … to … starboard."'

Immediately, everyone on the bridge was galvanized. Pankhurst grabbed the signal lamp to acknowledge *Moorsom*'s signal. Sub-Lieutenant Wainwright disappeared down the companionway, sliding his hands down the side rails with his feet not so much as touching the steps. Lt Haliley grabbed for a pair of binoculars hanging above the chart table.

'Sound action stations!' Whitfield ordered. He turned to Ted. 'Starboard bridge lookout!'

'Aye, sir!' Ted snapped in response.

Running across the bridge, Ted began to scan the sea ahead. The surface was grey and broken by small, chopping waves. Pankhurst appeared at his side, faced towards the stern and started to relay the warning signal to HMS *Nestor*, the next destroyer back in the line. The shutters in the signal lamp clacked with a rapid urgency as Pankhurst sent the signal in Morse code.

Ted was afraid he might not see the mine: he was not quite sure what it would look like. However, after only a few minutes, he spied something smooth and round and black, with stalks like feelers sticking out from it, bobbing in the sea and coming up fast.

'Mine sighted off the starboard bow, sir!' he shouted, pointing at the object.

'Two degrees to port,' Whitfield commanded. The helmsman turned the ship's wheel to give her more distance from the mine.

Haliley swung his binoculars in the direction of Ted's arm and said, 'Sighting confirmed, sir.' He then leaned over the edge of the bridge and yelled, 'Mine ten degrees off the starboard bow!'

Below on the foredeck, under the command of Wainwright, six ratings stood at the ready with rifles. As *Nomad* came abreast of the mine, all the sailors opened fire on it. For ten tense seconds, there was a chatter of spasmodic rifle fire. Small splashes erupted around the mine, which continued to bob menacingly on the surface.

Suddenly, Wainwright snatched one of the rifles from a rating, slamming a cartridge into the breach. Taking careful aim, he fired a single shot. There was a massive, crumping explosion that made Ted jump. The sea rose in a dense white column twenty metres high, spray drifted over *Nomad*'s decks and the windows of the bridge rattled.

'Resume course,' Whitfield said calmly as everyone on the bridge returned to their positions. 'And well spotted, boy,' he continued, smiling briefly at Ted who felt himself puff up inside with pride.

As dusk fell on the following day, *Nomad* slowed and veered west into the Firth of Forth. With the lights of the city of Edinburgh off the port beam, she sailed under the Forth Bridge and tied up to a buoy off a large naval dockyard. Alongside lay a number of massive warships. Those members of the crew not on duty lined the ship's rail to look at the sight.

'Will you just take a look at that!' Pankhurst exclaimed with a hint of awe in his voice as Ted joined him by the aft torpedo tube. 'That's the Battlecruiser Fleet and the 5th Battle Squadron.'

'Which battleship is which?' Ted asked.

'They're not battleships,' Pankhurst explained. 'They're battlecruisers, faster and lighter on their toes. The one on the end is HMS *Lion*. She's Vice-Admiral Sir David Beatty's flagship. Astern of her is HMS *Indefatigable*, then HMS *Queen Mary*.' He pointed to a vessel moored to another buoy. 'Further off is HMS *Engadine*. You know what she is?' He did not wait for Ted's answer. 'She's a new sort of ship, an aircraft carrier. Look at her stern.'

By the last light of the day, Ted could just make out the flat deck behind the ungainly bulk of the hangar. Upon it, a seaplane was silhouetted against the sky.

The following afternoon, Ted was busy polishing the silver in the officers' wardroom when he heard a pinnace pull alongside followed by the shrill whistle of the bo'sun's pipe.

'Captain's back,' Catchpole announced. 'He'll have

our sailing orders. Make the most of the view of green and bonnie Scotland, boy,' he added, jutting his head in the direction of the porthole through which a weak spring sun was shining. 'You'll see nowt but grey waves and white tops for a while.'

Half an hour later, Ted stood with the rest of his mess, mustered before Lt Haliley, their divisional officer.

'This is what you've all been waiting to hear,' he addressed them. 'The Admiralty has intercepted German Telefunken signals and these indicate that the German High Seas Fleet is about to set sail from Wilhelmshaven, heading out into the North Sea. We are to join up with Admiral Jellicoe's Grand Fleet near Jutland Bank, off the coast of Denmark, and head the enemy off.' He paused and looked round the gathered ratings. 'Any questions?'

A few of Ted's mess-mates exchanged glances but, to Ted's discomfort, no one spoke. He had a question but he was afraid to voice it in case it made him look foolish. On the other hand, the Chief had said asking was learning. He summoned his courage and put his hand up. Everyone looked at him and he felt himself beginning to blush bright red.

'Well, speak up,' Haliley ordered.

'Please, sir,' he asked as if he were still in the village school at Clovelly rather than on board one of His Majesty's warships, 'what's a Telefunken?'

'The wireless,' Haliley replied. 'We listen in to their transmissions and decipher them. Now –' he turned to face the gathering – 'we sail at 23:00. May God bless us and guide us all.'

The remainder of the afternoon was spent refuelling

Nomad from an oil lighter, replenishing stores and making certain that everything was shipshape. In the mess, whatever was loose was stowed away, while in the wardroom all the crockery was packed into cupboards and the bottles of wine and spirits were returned to a locked box in the galley. Knots in ropes were tested or retied, gun mountings were re-greased.

Ted was given the task of ensuring that the Carley floats, oblong blocks of cork and canvas about three metres long, were loose in their frames. He could not understand, when everything else was being secured, why these had to be free. When he asked Sharkey, he was told not to tempt fate.

'But what are they?' Ted persisted.

'Life rafts,' Sharkey replied soberly.

At exactly eleven o'clock that night, as six bells sounded, *Nomad* slipped her moorings and, making a tight turn, sailed out beneath the Forth Bridge. Ted stood at the stern, watching the land begin to slip away into the night. Through the girders of the bridge, he could hear the rumble of a night mail train heading south for Edinburgh.

In his mind's eye, he saw it travelling down a map of England, to Newcastle and York where, in complete disregard for the railway network, it veered south-west until it steamed into the station on the hills above Clovelly. His mother and father stood on the platform. They were waving to him as he stepped off the train, with a medal pinned upon his chest. His face was bearded under his sailor's cap around the brim of which were the words HMS *Nomad*, shining as brightly as new-forged gold.

By dawn, *Nomad* was steaming in convoy with what appeared to be a veritable armada. Ted was on watch on the fo'c'sle, and wherever he looked there was a warship, grey against the sea. The sky was streaked with thin trails of smoke from their funnels. Every now and then, the aircraft he had seen on HMS *Engadine* flew over, reconnoitring ahead.

At midday, when he served the officers their lunch, he found them in a subdued mood. Only Whitfield made any real attempt at conversation and then it was only small talk. Ted could feel the tension in the air.

As he and Catchpole were clearing away the plates from the main course, there came an urgent knock on the wardroom door. It was Pankhurst.

'I've just caught a German wireless message, sir,' he told Whitfield. 'Signal strength very strong, sir.'

For a moment, the officers were silent, then Whitfield, removing his napkin and folding it slowly, almost fastidiously, said, 'I think, gentlemen, this may be a day that will go down in history.'

Just after two o'clock, the order was given to clear for action. Ted joined the gun crew. The weapon was made ready for firing. No one spoke except to give a curt order. The wind was cold against Ted's face. The sea was running with a light swell. A fine spray blew across him, stinging his skin and making his eyes water. He tried to empty his mind of everything but the task ahead, handing shells to Sharkey for him to prime and hand on. Time seemed to stand still, the tick of seconds replaced by the thud of waves as *Nomad* ploughed, at speed, through the swell.

After what seemed an eternity, someone pointed to the east and exclaimed, 'That's them!'

Ted stared into the distance. Lining the horizon was a row of small, dark smudges. No sooner had he seen the ships than he heard a muffled thunder, like a storm rumbling its way through a range of distant mountains. Yet this was no storm. The battlecruisers up ahead of *Nomad* had opened fire with their main armaments, guns with barrels over ten metres long that could fire a shell a distance of twenty kilometres. With every salvo, the smoke belched out of the barrels, some of them forming massive smoke rings that drifted on the breeze, slowly fading away. No sooner had the guns roared than the German High Seas Fleet returned fire. Huge columns of water erupted a kilometre off the line of battlecruisers.

'When do we open fire?' Ted asked, speaking his thoughts out loud.

'Not yet,' Sharkey replied. 'Let the big bulldogs have their fight before us little terriers nip in.'

Nomad increased speed. Astern of HMS *Nestor*, with *Nicator* behind her, she headed for the line of battlecruisers. Then, steering a course through it, she sailed along the line, between the two competing navies. As *Nomad* passed in front of the great ships, their massive guns seemed to shake the very atoms of the air. Yet this was not what scared Ted. The German ships were getting their range. Their shells, exploding in the sea, were getting nearer and nearer. Already, they were scoring the occasional hit on a British vessel.

'Only a matter of time …' Sharkey said ominously, to no one in particular.

No sooner had Sharkey spoken than there was a gigantic explosion. The sky abreast of *Nicator* reverberated. A whirling maelstrom of black smoke, grey spume and dull, orange flames billowed upwards for hundreds of metres. As the shock wave of the explosion travelled over the sea, Ted could track its progress as an invisible force flattening the tops of the waves. When it reached *Nomad*, it struck him like a sudden strong blast.

'Oh, sweet Lord!' a voice exclaimed. 'That's *Indefatigable*.'

'Was,' said another voice, laconically.

The smoke rose higher and higher, expanding over the sea as if it would darken and choke the whole sky. Pieces of the battlecruiser began raining down, huge plates of steel spiralling downwards like leaves in autumn, smaller shards plummeting into the sea. A small steam pinnace, hurled high into the air, came down almost intact only to break into smithereens on impact. *Nicator* veered sharply but did not lose speed.

Ted felt himself starting to shiver. He could not tell why. He was not cold. Sharkey put his hand on his shoulder and said, 'Don't fret yourself, lad. They never knew what happened. Pray God it'll be that swift for us.'

Sharkey's words ran a sharp blade of fear along Ted's spine. It occurred to him that he had just seen a thousand men die in a cataclysm of fire and high explosive and he realized that, at a moment's notice, that could also be his fate. He did not want to die. This was not why he had joined the Navy. He wanted to fight, but not to be injured or be killed. The urge rose in him to find someone and ask if he might, please, be excused, like he had in the village school. But this was not school and there was no way out. He was in this until the end.

The gun crew started cheering. On the horizon, there was another column of smoke.

'That's got Fritz!' exclaimed the gun layer. The words were hardly out of his mouth when there was another sky-shattering explosion. A German salvo had struck the battlecruiser HMS *Queen Mary*. The cheering stopped abruptly as a chain of explosions travelled along the length of her hull, ripping her open.

A signal lamp flashed on HMS *Lion,* which was also coming under heavy fire.

'This is it,' remarked Sharkey, bluntly.

Ted tried to read the Morse code but it was too quick for him.

'What does it say?' he asked.

'Engage the enemy,' Sharkey answered as he produced his roll of lint and handed two pieces to Ted. 'Time to earn medals, lad,' he continued. 'Or not, as the case may be,' he added ominously.

'How long do you think it'll last?' Ted said as he folded the lint and pushed it in his ears.

Sharkey pulled a silver half-hunter watch out of his pocket, snapped the lid open and replied, 'It's half-past four. Tea time.' He paused and stared at the watch. 'This was my gran'dad's watch. He was a railway guard, he was.' He closed it and put it back in his pocket. 'No telling how long it'll last but you mark my words –' he put his hand once more upon Ted's shoulder, his fingers tightening – 'it'll be the shortest piece of time in your life.'

The three destroyers turned in a line and steamed at full speed for the enemy. Astern, the wake curved in a white arc as if *Nomad* were tearing the sea apart. The gun crew readied themselves for action, the sightsetters checking the calibration for the umpteenth time, the trainer moving the gun on her mounting as if to reassure himself there was sufficient grease to keep the cogs meshing smoothly.

Ted looked at the ammunition lift. The first shell they would fire at the German Navy was there, ready to be loaded. Ted ran his fingers along the brass casing of the shell, as if introducing himself to it. It was cold and slick and polished and, for a moment, he wondered where that pointed projectile at the end would go, what it would hit, which ship it might sink or how many men it might kill.

Where Bellingham's voice came from, Ted could not tell. Despite the stuffing in his ears, it seemed to fill the entire world with just two words – 'Open fire!'

Ted swung the shell towards Sharkey. One of the sightsetters shouted the estimated distance to the target and Sharkey turned the ring on the apex of the shell to set the fuse. Ted watched as the shell slid into the breech and the breech block closed. The gunlayer pulled on the firing cord. The body of the gun recoiled. As the breech block was swung open again, the brass shell case automatically ejected, clattering and bouncing on the deck. Sharkey kicked it to one side. Ted turned. There was another shell on the lift, ready for him.

'Let's have it!' shouted Sharkey.

Ted, without thinking, obeyed.

A shell exploded in the sea a hundred metres off the

stern. The spray drifted in the air like the pollen of an evil flower. Oblivious to it, Ted and the crew continued to fire, altering the trajectory a few degrees with each round. By the tenth shell, Ted realized in a detached way that he was working like an unquestioning automaton, like a dancer in some contorted, bizarre ballet. His actions fitted into a rhythm with Sharkey and the others, a part of the cruel choreography of war.

'We're going about!' a voice yelled. Ted was only just able to discern it through the wadding in his ears.

Sharkey leaned towards Ted and, putting his mouth close to his ear, shouted, 'We'll hold our fire for a bit.' Despite his lips almost brushing Ted's face, he sounded as if he was speaking from far away.

'Why?' Ted shouted. Even his own voice seemed distant and indistinct.

'It's the turn of the tin fish,' Sharkey replied enigmatically and he jutted his chin for'ard towards where the torpedo crews were readying for action. As the aft tube moved out to its firing position at right angles to *Nomad*'s hull, Ted could see the bulbous end of the torpedo filling the dark interior of the barrel.

The three destroyers were halfway through their change of course when *Nomad* noticeably began to lose speed. *Nicator* sped past, her funnel pumping smoke.

Puzzled and afraid, Ted shouted, 'What's happening? Have we been hit?'

'Beats me,' Sharkey shrugged.

The first torpedo was fired. The long cylinder shot from the tube to splash horizontally on the choppy sea, quickly burying its nose in the waves and disappearing. The last thing Ted saw of it was the propeller at the back spinning in a blur, biting into the water and leaving a trail of bubbles that quickly dispersed.

At the moment the second torpedo was fired, there was a single high-pitched whine that grew to a crescendo, then abruptly faded to be immediately followed by a massive thump. The air seemed to contract, the sea rose as if an invisible giant had smashed his hand on the surface and Ted and the others were instantaneously drenched.

As the air cleared, Sharkey raised his arm. Approaching at speed, and closing fast, was a line of eight German destroyers. Puffs of smoke erupting over their bows indicated they were opening fire with their for'ard armament.

No orders had to be given. The trainer swung the gun round on its mounting. The sightsetters lowered the elevation of the barrel. Ted reached for a shell. Sharkey glanced at the oncoming enemy vessels. He didn't need to know the distance to set the fuses: it was changing all the time. And shortening.

Within a few minutes, it seemed as if *Nomad* was the only ship in the battle. All around her, shells erupted in the sea, obscuring *Nicator* and *Nestor* in clouds of spray and spume. The reports of the firing gun and the din of explosions deafened Ted but it did not matter. He knew what his role was and he did it with his mind somehow switched off from the realities of the danger surrounding him.

Suddenly, the deck under Ted's feet shivered and rippled as if it were made of cardboard. A blast of searing air scorched his cheeks and threw him against Sharkey who stumbled and only stayed on his feet by grasping hold of the breech mechanism lever of the gun.

Where the aft torpedo tube had been, thick oily smoke was belching from a jagged hole in the deck plates. Halfway between the hole and Ted lay the body of a sailor. Twitching spasmodically, it was missing an arm and its head. Ted stared at it then turned away, feeling the bitter rush of bile rising to his throat. He fought the vomit coursing up through his body.

There was another screech and a second shell ripped through *Nomad* amidships. Again, the destroyer shuddered like a huge animal receiving a mortal blow: then, a jet of super-heated steam plumed up out of the belly of the ship like a geyser.

Ted pulled the lint out of his ears. Apart from the hissing of the steam, the world was curiously silent. Yet what scared him most was the stillness of the deck. Usually, night and day, he could feel the gentle, reassuring vibration of *Nomad*'s generators and turbines turning. Now there was only the movement of the sea rocking her.

'She's stopped,' observed the gunlayer, confirming what Ted already knew.

'Fritz is sailing off!' exclaimed one of the sightsetters.

Ted looked up. Sure enough, the German destroyers were turning.

'Just as well,' remarked the gunlayer. 'We're a sitting duck wallowing here.'

Sharkey looked at his watch.

'Twenty-one minutes,' he said.

After a few moments of calm, there was sudden

pandemonium. The Chief appeared running along the deck, yelling. His words were indistinct against the hiss of the steam and the boom of *Nicator's* guns which were firing at the disappearing enemy destroyers. It was only as he drew nearer that his orders became audible.

'Man the pumps!' the Chief hollered. 'Man the pumps!' He caught sight of Ted. 'You! Report to the bridge! And mind the steam. It's hot enough to flay you.'

Avoiding the gaping hole and hissing steam, Ted ran as fast as he could to the bridge, where he found Pankhurst watching another British destroyer sailing past at speed. An Aldis signal lamp flashed from her bridge.

'*Nicator* asks, "Do you need assistance?", sir,' Pankhurst reported to Lt Cmdr Whitfield.

'Make, "No. Continue on your course,"' the Captain replied.

As Pankhurst raised his own signal lamp, the shutters clicking out their message, Whitfield saw Ted standing at the top of the companionway.

'You come with me, boy,' he said curtly. 'Step lively.'

Ted followed the Captain down to his cabin. There, the officer opened a safe and started removing heavy ledgers and leather-bound books. He piled them on a small writing desk, knocking aside a blotter and a silver and crystal glass ink well, which fell to shatter on the cabin floor, spilling its contents.

'In the drawer under my bunk ...' Whitfield continued.

Tugging the drawer open, Ted found a canvas bag

with leather straps and buckles. He was surprised to find it was heavy, with lead weights sewn into the seams.

'Hold it open.'

Ted obeyed. Whitfield started sliding the contents of the safe into it.

'Confidential papers,' the Captain explained. 'Code books, ciphers, signals, ship's orders. They must not fall into the hands of the enemy. Now,' he said, placing the last book in the bag and fastening the buckles, 'go to the ship's side and toss it overboard. Then report to the bridge.'

The bag was heavy but Ted succeeded in getting it to the ship's rail. He laid it on the deck then, kneeling, pushed it over the side. It fell and hit the water, floating for a few seconds before rapidly sinking. Ted watched it vanish into the murky grey sea. As he rose to his feet, he happened to glance at the horizon. What he saw made the hairs on his neck prickle and froze his muscles. A German battleship was heading straight for *Nomad*.

'Take cover!' a voice yelled at him from above. 'Take cover!'

Ted looked up. Pankhurst was gesticulating at him from the bridge.

The first shell struck *Nomad* at the stern and the impact rocked her over. Ted lost his footing and slid across the deck to end up against a bulkhead. The second took off the top of the middle funnel. The third cut the mainmast, which crashed on to the deck, surrounding him with a tangle of cables and splintered wood.

All thought was eradicated from Ted's mind. He hunkered down close to the bulkhead and covered his head with his arms. Yet another shell struck *Nomad* just above the water-line. She lurched and began to list. A hand grabbed him by the arm and roughly hauled him to his feet. It was Pankhurst.

There was a flash of high explosive near the bow. *Nomad* lurched another degree or two and began to settle in the water. The deck plates creaked and squealed as if the ship were in pain.

'She's going down!' Pankhurst shouted over the tumult of the barrage. 'Take your boots off.'

Puzzled, Ted did as he was told, noticing that Pankhurst was standing in his socks.

'Put this on,' Pankhurst ordered, thrusting a Miranda lifejacket into Ted's hands.

Again, he obeyed, tying the ribbons at his waist.

Finally, Pankhurst said, 'Give me your hand.'

They stepped towards the ship's side. The rail had been blown away.

'Ready, ship's boy?' Pankhurst asked.

Ted looked up at Pankhurst. His face was drawn but he managed a wink.

'Ready, Leading Hand,' Ted answered.

Together, hand in hand, they jumped.

PART TWO

DECEMBER 1916 TO MARCH 1917

'Swim!' It was Pankhurst. 'Swim! If we're too close when she goes down, we'll be sucked under with her.'

Ted tried. His arms were heavy.

'I'm tuckered out.' Now it was Sharkey speaking, his words little more than a murmur.

'Hang on, shipmate,' said another lost voice. 'Won't be long. If you sleep, you die.'

Over the sound of the sea in his ears, a voice chided Ted, saying, 'Foley! For heaven's sake, boy, make the effort!' It was his old teacher from the village school.

'Yes, miss,' Ted replied, without thinking.

Ted felt himself go limp. The water rushed into his mouth, the raw salt burning the sides of his throat, searing through his lungs like a firebrand. He kicked with his feet. Over his head, he could see the underneath of a ship's hull, dense and black against the light of day.

The bubbles leaking from between Ted's lips pirouetted towards the surface above. He reached out for them, to cram them back into his mouth, but they broke in his fingers like mercury. His lungs were bursting and his head was throbbing to the drum of his beating heart. A fish swam by. It seemed to have a mocking smile on its face. His terror mounted. It was no good. The weight of his clothing was dragging him down. He was growing colder by the second and he knew he was drowning.

Something shook him, gently. Perhaps, he thought, it was the hand of death itself.

'Make the effort,' another voice whispered.

Ted sat bolt upright. The hull of the ship was now the wooden planks of the barrack ceiling and he was cold because, although he had slept with his clothing on, it was freezing outside and the coarse German Army blanket had slipped off him during the night. The dry straw in his palliasse, the thin, cotton-covered mattress upon which he slept, rustled with his every movement.

'Only a dream,' murmured the voice.

Glancing down from his bunk, the topmost tier of three, Ted could just make out the face of Bob Lowry in the gloom. Dawn had only just broken and little more than the tiniest glimmer of daylight showed through the thick sacking curtain covering the window.

'Time to shake a leg,' Bob whispered, moving off into the semi-darkness.

Gradually, as Ted woke more fully, it all came back to him. *Nomad* was gone. He could hear, somewhere in the back of his mind, the rattle of chains and loose gear within her as her bow rose vertically and she slid stern first beneath the grey waves.

How long he had floated in the sea, Ted could not tell. It was at least several hours. Pankhurst had stayed close by, encouraging him. Ted was a good swimmer but, gradually, he grew exhausted. The lifejacket was bulky and, although it provided some buoyancy, it made swimming awkward and an effort. Every now and then, a wave broke over his head, forcing him under the water and causing him to panic, to use up more precious energy. He could almost feel his will to live ebbing away.

Eventually, Ted and Pankhurst had been pulled from the sea by the crew of a German torpedo boat. They had removed his lifejacket, wrapped him in a sheet of tarpaulin and given him a cup of hot water and a bun that tasted of onions. Now he was held in a prisoner-of-war camp near Brandenburg, forty miles west of Berlin near the banks of the River Havel.

Gently lowering himself to the floor, so as not to disturb the two men sleeping in the bunks beneath his own, Ted tugged on his boots. Of German military issue, they were a bit tight but of good quality leather which he had made supple and waterproof by rubbing lard into them. Once they were laced up, he tiptoed softly down the barrack towards the door. The lard also prevented them from squeaking.

The barrack was a long, low, wooden building with a gently pitched roof, erected on brick piles like stilts, about a metre off the ground. Along each side were three small windows, the only door at one end. The walls were lined with ranks of triple bunks. Halfway down was a living area containing four large deal tables, some benches and a storage cupboard made by the inmates from boxes. In the centre of the tables was a large pot-bellied stove with a galvanized steel chimney rising to the roof, the upper half smoke-blackened from a crack in the casing.

There was no other furniture, no pictures or drawings or anything else to bring colour to the place, although there was, near the cupboard, a shelf bearing a few books leaning haphazardly against each other. Some of the bunks had small wooden boxes nailed to the frame to hold the occupant's scanty personal possessions. Those who had more clothes than they could wear at once kept them folded flat under their palliasses.

Bob was waiting by the door. He was a ship's boy from a merchant vessel sunk by a mine.

'Ready?' he asked.

'As I'll ever be,' Ted replied, hunching his shoulders and tugging his coat collar close about his throat.

Bob turned the handle and swung the door open. A blast of icy wind struck them in the face, bringing tears to their eyes. During the night, more snow had fallen and the camp was covered in a layer twenty centimetres thick, untrammelled as yet by a single footstep. Not even the sentries had ventured out for, after the snow, the sky had cleared and the temperature had plunged.

'What do you think?' Ted asked.

'Minus ten,' Bob answered, 'and falling.'

They set off down the wooden steps and across the snow, their boots crunching on the frozen surface. There was no sign of any other living human being. Even the guard towers along the barbed wire perimeter fence were empty. No one, the Germans knew, would try to escape in this weather. Only one building showed any sign of activity and that was restricted to a wisp of smoke being snatched from the chimney by the wind.

'Bacon and eggs,' Ted said as they approached the building, 'and fried mushrooms.'

'Boiled eggs, with soldiers of bread and butter,' Bob rejoined. 'And toast with orange marmalade.'

They reached the door and stopped. Together, they sniffed the air.

'Kippers?' mused Ted.

'Nope!' said Bob.

They looked at each other and chorused, 'Stodge.'

Inside the cookhouse, the air was welcomingly damp and warm. Clouds of steam filled the place. On a row of stoves simmered large pans of oat porridge, their sides scorched by flames and heat. At a table stood the day's cook, a burly man with a palm tree tattooed on his arm. In its shade lay a semi-naked Polynesian girl in a grass skirt.

'Morning, lads!' he greeted them. 'Hut?'

'Seven,' Ted answered.

The cook studied a list pinned to the table and shouted, 'Hut 7! One hundred and sixteen poor muckers that've got themselves locked up courtesy of Kaiser Bill.'

From within the clouds of steam, a voice shouted back, ''Ut 7, 'undred an' sixteen. Aye!' to be followed by a man appearing dressed in the remnants of a sailor's uniform and carrying two large wooden buckets filled to the brim with porridge. He lowered them to the floor.

'Here you are,' said the cook. 'Nosh for Hut 7. On your way.' Ted picked up one bucket and Bob the other. 'Look lively,' he added, holding the door open for them. 'Tastes like slop and sawdust when it's cold.'

The buckets were heavy and carrying them through the snow was not easy but eventually they reached the barrack and entered to find most of the occupants up and waiting, mess tins and spoons at the ready. The lengths of sacking, which served as curtains and kept in what warmth there was within the building, still hung in place. Several oil lamps had been lit, giving the barrack a warm glow to which the mica window in the stove added its contribution. The embers from the night before had been coaxed into life and a huge black kettle on the hob was already close to boiling. The air was beginning to get smoky from the crack in the chimney pipe.

Ted and Bob lifted their buckets on to one of the tables and the occupants of the barrack lined up behind them. As was customary, those who had fetched the food were given their portion first. Ted shook two dollops of the porridge into a mess tin and, taking his spoon from his pocket, went to sit on one of the benches.

There was an advantage to being among the first served: the heavier porridge sank to the bottom of the bucket so those who took from the top had something that was slightly more liquid and easier to swallow. Those who came later would have to dilute theirs with hot water. Even so, Ted found it hard to get down. He wished he could have added a little milk, or a spoonful of sugar, as his mother would have done.

When their breakfast was finished, the prisoners set about preparing for their day. A few were on camp duties, which meant they would spend the next ten hours cleaning the German officers' quarters, waiting on them or standing by in the *Kommandant*'s office to run errands. Most of the men, however, could look forward to another day of enforced boredom and the fight to alleviate it.

After completing his share of the barrack chores, sweeping out the floor and returning the buckets to the cookhouse, Ted tidied his bunk. At eight o'clock, a German guard slammed open the door and shouted, '*Raus! Raus! Appell! Appell!*' to which the prisoners responded with a caustic chorus of 'Rats! Rats! And apples to you!' They nevertheless obeyed this order and filed out for the daily head-count, forming ranks on the parade ground before the *Kommandant*'s building, stamping their feet and hugging their arms about their chests to combat the cold.

When the Germans were satisfied there was no one unaccounted for, the prisoners were dismissed. Some, who were forced to work in a railway yard shovelling coal into locomotive tenders, lined up by the main camp gate while others set off to the far end of the compound where they were engaged in building three new barracks. Ted headed in the direction of Hut 16.

Larger than most of the other barracks, Hut 16 was the camp recreation building. Consisting of a large hall, it had a small stage at one end, a very battered and out of tune grand piano, some shelves of dog-eared books, a cupboard for stage props and a collection of benches fashioned out of rough-sawn planks.

The building was deserted as Ted entered. He moved some of the benches into a semi-circle then, from the back of the stage, carried out a blackboard which he set up on an easel pulled out from under the piano.

'Good morning, Ted,' a voice greeted him from the door. 'You're keen for a touch of teaching this morning.'

Ted turned. Walking across the hall was Pankhurst.

'Good morning, Leading Hand,' Ted replied, adding, 'it's my turn this week to set up.'

'So it is,' Pankhurst said. 'But, remember, I'm not Leading Hand. Not presently. We're not in the mess now. In *a* mess, sure enough, but not *the* mess. Our mess,' he went on ruefully, 'is home for fishes.'

'It just seems strange calling you George,' Ted admitted, opening the cupboard and placing a box of chalk and a rag on the floor by the blackboard.

'Well, that's what I am until we get us another berth on one of His Majesty's ships.' Pankhurst opened the lid of the piano and ran his hand along the keys. 'I think we should ask Fritz for a tuning fork and a spanner. I don't see how he can claim they're –' he put on a stagey German accent – '*inztrumentz ov ezcaping.*'

Ted grinned. 'Maybe I should call you Sir,' he suggested. 'Like a teacher.'

'Not yet,' Pankhurst answered, returning the grin. 'When I'm an officer with a bit of gold scrambled egg on the peak of my cap you can but, right now, George'll do. I'm not an officer and,' he added with a grimace, 'I'm certainly no schoolmaster.'

As Ted put slates out on the benches and placed a

small stick of chalk on each one, other prisoners began to arrive, chattering and laughing as if they were in the playground of a school somewhere in the heart of England. Aged between fourteen and sixteen, they had served upon a variety of vessels as ship's boy of one sort or another. Their other common denominator was that they had all been sunk, rescued and taken prisoner by the German Navy.

'Settle down, lads,' Pankhurst ordered. 'To your places.'

The boys fell silent and stood by the benches. Pankhurst positioned himself in front of the piano and commenced playing the national anthem. As the first bars unmelodiously clanked out of the piano, they all stood to attention and sang 'God Save the King'. Through the grimy window behind the piano, Ted could see heavy snowflakes gyrating lazily down to pile up on the sill. This formality over, Pankhurst closed the piano, took up a stick of chalk and wrote *Moorings* on the blackboard.

'Today,' he began, turning to face his class, 'we start learning how you moor a ship. With a horse, it's easy. You tie his nose to a tree or a fence. With a ship, it's not that simple. With a ship, you have to tether both nose and tail. We'll start with a simple-clump mooring. It consists of a buoy attached to a clump ...'

For the next hour and a half, the boys sat with their heads bowed, listening to Pankhurst's instruction, copying down his diagrams and words on their slates, reading them to themselves to learn them. At the end of the lesson, Pankhurst questioned them in depth then, finally, announced that that was all for the morning. Bob Lowry, whose turn it was to 'take down', stacked the benches and put away the blackboard, easel and slates. Ted, relieved of these chores, left Hut 16 and, with his collar turned up against the falling snow, made his way towards the camp carpenters' shop.

Built so that the prisoners could erect their own barracks and make or repair the camp furniture, the carpentry shop was also permitted to be used for prisoners' recreation. It was well stocked with woodworking tools but, as these had a definite potential as aids to escaping, they were overseen by a retired German cavalry officer called *Rittmeister* Götting.

He stood guard by the locked steel cupboard, handing the tools out one by one and counting them back in like a teacher distributing and collecting pencils. If so much as one tiny awl was missing, no one could leave until it was accounted for.

As Ted entered, the scents of sawn wood, linseed, smoke from the sawdust-burning stove and pine sap wafted over him. Beside the tool cupboard, *Rittmeister* Götting was sitting on a stool reading a book. At the far end, standing at a workbench was Dan Copley. A elderly, softly spoken seaman, he had been the chippy on HMS *Turbulent*. Ninety of his comrades lost their lives when she too was sunk during the battle which saw the end of *Nomad*.

'You're back then,' Copley commented as Ted approached him, his feet rustling through a drift of shavings. 'Can't keep you away. Still,' he continued, 'you're a wise lad. We all got a lot of hours to while away in this place. You make the most of them.'

Ted smiled and replied, 'I just don't like to do nothing.'

Going to a cupboard at the end of the workshop, Ted slowly opened the doors. The shelves were loaded with various semi-completed objects – a pair of bookends, a pen stand, a dressing table box with *Love to Dearest Sylvia from Brandenburg PoW Camp: 1916* crudely burned on to it with a red-hot poker – which other prisoners were either half-heartedly making or had given up on to pursue other time-passing activities. On the bottom shelf was a large object covered with a length of hessian.

As his fingers touched the cloth, Ted felt a surge of mixed emotions run through him. Sadness and longing mingled with excitement and expectation, the sort of anticipation he had felt at home, at Christmas, as his father handed him his present, wrapped in paper and tied with cord. He pulled the sacking free to reveal a half-constructed model boat about a metre long. Lifting it out of the cupboard, he placed it at the other end of the bench from where Dan was working.

'She's looking well,' Dan said. 'Who is she?'

Ted was silent for a moment then answered, 'She's going to be the *Evelyn*.'

'Pretty name,' Dan remarked.

'That's my mum's name,' Ted replied, a lump rising in his throat. 'My dad's fishing boat's named after her.'

Going to *Rittmeister* Götting, Ted collected a spoke-shave and began gently stroking wafer-thin slivers of wood off the side.

When he had first arrived in Brandenburg, Ted and the other prisoners in his detail had been addressed by two officers. The first was the German *Kommandant*. Wearing a smart uniform and riding boots, and carrying a crop in his right hand, he had stood on a small wooden platform at the end of the parade square with two junior officers positioned before him. With his hands clasped firmly behind his back, he had shouted at them.

'Now,' he had bellowed, 'you are all prisoners of the war, prisoners of His Majesty, Kaiser Wilhelm. You will behave yourselves. There will be no monking or lorking about.'

The prisoners had exchanged puzzled glances which turned into surreptitious grins when they realized he meant monkeying and larking about.

'You will not attempt the escape,' he continued. 'If you attempt the escape, no quarter will be given. You will be shot.'

The final word rang out like the report of a rifle, emphasized by the riding crop snapping against the side of his riding boot. It sent a frisson of terror up Ted's spine.

'So you will be good boys,' the *Kommandant* concluded. His voice softened a little and took on the tone of a benevolent if strict headmaster addressing an assembly of new and potentially naughty pupils. 'If you are good, you will see the German people will be kind. If you are bad, we shall punish you. Now you are dismiss.'

With these last words, he stepped down off the platform and marched stiffly away towards the camp administrative building, followed by his two junior officers.

The second officer to speak to Ted had been Commander Stannard. The senior prisoner of war in the camp he was, in contrast to the *Kommandant*, wearing a dark-blue Royal Navy serge uniform jacket with tarnished gold rings on the sleeves, a darned hole in one elbow and frayed cuffs. He had not stood on a dais but had sat on the end of a table in one of the barracks while several other prisoners kept watch at the door and windows.

'Right, chaps,' Stannard had said in a voice little louder than a whisper. 'Notwithstanding what Herr Fritz has said to you, I must remind you that it is the duty of every prisoner to attempt to escape. You know this as well as I do. However, escape from Brandenburg is, frankly, well nigh impossible. We reckon we're more than four hundred miles from the German coast and then you've still got the North Sea between us and dear old Blighty. So –' he paused to let his words sink in – 'our situation looks pretty hopeless and, I don't deny, it is.'

One of the lookouts had hissed at that point and the Commander stopped speaking until the all-clear was given.

'Not one of us,' he then continued, 'stands a snowball's chance in hell if he doesn't have maps, money and a good disguise – never mind being able to speak German.'

As he addressed the prisoners, Ted became increasingly depressed. The war had already been going on for two years and there was no end to it in sight. The armies were at stalemate in the trenches and mud of Flanders and neither the British nor the Imperial German navies seemed to have the upper hand at sea.

'So my advice to you is to make the best of a bad thing,' Commander Stannard had finally suggested. 'Try not to brood upon your situation. There is little you can do about it. At least at present ...'

For the first three or four months of his imprisonment, Ted had managed to push all thoughts of escape to the back of his mind. There had been too much else to do. The prisoners had spent the summer months playing cricket matches among themselves, growing vegetables in the plots between the huts and swimming in the small lake around which the camp was built.

They had also removed the boards from their bunks and scrubbed them down to combat bed bugs, chopped firewood or broke coal and patched up the barracks, filling any cracks with tar in readiness for the long, bitter German winter. Several theatrical productions were staged in Hut 16, including *Julius Caesar*, in which Ted played the minor role of a Roman legionnaire.

Once autumn came and the winter closed in, the prisoners' activities were curtailed. They spent little time out of doors and passed their waking hours in the barracks sewing, playing cards or draughts, talking and making souvenirs of their imprisonment out of whatever scrap they could acquire. One soldier made cigarette lighters out of brass rifle cartridge cases filched from the German guards; another carved little figures out of bottle corks; a third took to making abstract pictures out of ducks' feathers he had collected from the edge of the lake. And Ted started building the *Evelyn*.

Over the weeks, as he worked on her, Ted's thoughts returned to England and Clovelly. The more this happened through the colourless days of winter, the more he began to ponder the chances of escape. That he wanted to escape, he was certain. He yearned to see his parents, smell the hay fields and beech woods above Clovelly and hear the tide upon the foreshore, rattling the round pebbles together. On the other hand, he was conscious of the *Kommandant's* blunt warning which, in turn, scared him not from the fear of a bullet through his chest but the fact that that bullet would mean he would never see North Devon again.

Every three months, a consignment of parcels arrived in Brandenburg. Sent by the International Red Cross, they contained simple essential items and small luxuries for the prisoners of war. The Germans, under international law, permitted these to be distributed from the Parcels Office, a small hut not far from the camp main gate. The prisoners, under the watchful eye of a German officer called *Hauptmann* Vogel, organized the allocation of the parcels, taking it in turns to provide the work parties by sending two men from each barrack.

When, in February, three horse-drawn wagons driven by German soldiers trundled through the slush and mud to halt in front of the Parcels Office, it was Ted and Pankhurst's turn to represent their barrack on the work party.

One wall of the Parcels Office was piled to the

ceiling with cardboard boxes stencilled with a red cross. In the centre was a stove and a table. At one end sat Stoker 'Goody' Goodenough, the distribution clerk. At the other end sat *Hauptmann* Vogel. As the camp censor, it was his job to ensure the parcels contained nothing of use in an escape. His role was unnecessary for the Red Cross, being an impartial charity, never put contraband in their deliveries.

A German sentry stood by the door. He was a young man of about nineteen whom the prisoners had nicknamed Dot-and-Carry-One, because of his limp. He had a garish scar across his forehead and a hacking cough.

As each parcel was taken down, it was put on the table and opened by *Hauptmann* Vogel who then cursorily rummaged about in it before nodding his permission to proceed. It was then re-sealed and Goodenough, checking against a list, allocated it to a prisoner whose name he wrote on the lid.

'It's heavy work, heaving the boxes to and fro,' Pankhurst announced as they entered the Parcels Office. 'And it makes your mouth water.'

'What do you mean?' Ted asked. He had not done parcel duty before.

'You'll see,' Pankhurst said with a wink.

When *Hauptmann* Vogel opened the first parcel put on the table, Ted understood. It contained not only buttons and thread, tobacco and matches, woollen socks and mittens, a prayer book, packets of tea, coffee and sugar and a copy of Charles Dickens' *Oliver Twist*, but also a pocket-sized German–English dictionary bound in red leather, a slab of brittle toffee, two bars of chocolate, a packet of pear drops and a small tin of jam. The stove was well fired up and, as the parcels warmed, the aroma of chocolate and toffee was almost too much for Ted to bear.

At noon, a halt was called. *Hauptmann* Vogel departed for his midday meal, leaving the sentry to make sure no further parcels were dealt with in his absence. After two hours of lifting, opening, re-closing and re-stacking parcels, Ted's arms ached more than they had as a member of a gun crew.

'Who's for a cup of coffee?' Stoker Goodenough asked cheerily as soon as *Hauptmann* Vogel was out of earshot. 'You game, Fritz, my son?' he added, looking at the sentry. 'It's *ersatz*. Kaiser's coffee. Made of acorns. You're not having any of the real thing like what we got in these boxes.' He pointed to a chair. 'Pull up a pew, chum. Let your hoofs have a holiday.'

The sentry nodded and smiled but remained standing.

Ted picked up a dictionary from the nearest parcel and opened it, thumbing through to the section for *S*.

'Sick set zen,' he read out at last.

For a moment, Dot-and-Carry-One looked puzzled then he grinned broadly and replied, '*Sich setzen! Ya! Danke!*' He sat down, leaning his rifle against the wall.

'Was he in the trenches?' Ted enquired, rather pleased with himself at having managed to speak German and be understood.

'Yes, he was, poor blighter,' the stoker replied. 'And his injuries are worse than you can see. His lungs've had it. He was gassed. Mustard gas. You breathe it in and it eats into your lungs like acid. He'll not see his twenty-first birthday. The irony was it was German gas what did it. They released a cloud of it to blow over our lads, but the wind changed. Makes you glad you're a sailor, don't it?'

As the acorn coffee brewed, Pankhurst and Goodenough chatted to the sentry in broken German. Ted left the table and stood at the window, gazing out. The hut overlooked the main entrance to the camp. The gate consisted of a wooden frame with barbed wire cross-crossing it. At one side was a sentry box with a guard in it. Opposite this was the guardhouse, a wooden building about the size of the Parcels Office but with a small porch on the front, raised a little above the mud of the roadway.

It looked so easy. The gate was open to allow a cart to leave, carrying a pile of empty sacks and two barrels. Freedom was just a hundred metres away. If, Ted considered, he could get himself inside one of those barrels or under the pile of sacks, he'd be away.

Yet no sooner had the thought occurred to him than the sentry stopped the cart, looked in the barrels and, unsheathing his bayonet, prodded the sacks. Ted could almost feel the point of the blade jabbing him in the spine.

'Want your share of boiled burnt acorns?' Goodenough's voice cut into Ted's reverie. 'Milk and sugar?' he added dryly. 'One lump or two?'

Ted turned away from the window, a sense of disappointment niggling him. Escape was certainly not going to be that simple.

'Yes, please,' he said, 'milk and two lumps.'

He reached out for the mug of coffee. As always, it

was black and unsweetened and smelled like charred bark. Yet, as he sipped it, Ted's mind was detached. Escape was out of the question – for now. The vigilant sentry aside, it was mid-winter. He would not survive a night in the open, on the run, in sub-zero temperatures. But come the spring – that just might be a different matter altogether.

The week after Ted's duty day in the Parcels Office, the weather turned truly vicious. A blizzard howled down from the Baltic, driving the snow almost horizontally across the camp. In next to no time, it drifted up against the barracks, piling high against every north-facing wall until the ridge of the roof and the ground were joined by a slope of tightly packed snow and ice.

For three days, the temperature did not rise above –15°C. The stove in Hut 7 was barely able to warm the air around the tables, never mind at the far ends of the building. The prisoners slept in as many clothes as they could get on yet even this did not keep the cold at bay.

'Stone the crows!' muttered Bob, waking on the third morning of the blizzard and struggling to get his foot and three socks into his boot. It was so cold, the leather was rigid. The laces, which had been damp when he had been sitting round the stove the night before, were as stiff and pliable as twigs.

'Just as well it's not our turn for the galley,' Ted replied, looking down the barrack to where two other prisoners were hunching themselves into greatcoats in readiness for the trudge to the cook-house.

'The stodge'll be like half-set concrete by the time it gets here,' Bob remarked sullenly.

'All the more reason to get a shift on,' Ted answered.

He walked to the centre of the hut and put his hand on the side of the stove. It was cold. He slowly slid his fingers round it, keeping his palm flat to the metal. At the very back he felt what he was looking for. An area the size of the ball of his thumb was discernibly warm.

Bob stood over him and asked, 'Well?' in a tone which suggested he expected the worst but hoped for at least a thin sliver of luck.

'It's still in,' Ted grinned. 'I'll do the fire. It's your turn to get the water.'

Bob shrugged. 'The tap'll be frozen again,' he remarked, morosely adding, 'I'll have to get snow.' This, he knew, meant more than one trip out into the blizzard. It took four bucketsful of snow to provide one of water by the time it was melted down in the kettle.

Very carefully, Ted opened the stove door and, with his bare hands, started to rake the ash out on to the heat-buckled tin tray upon which the stove stood. Every time his fingers came in contact with a piece of blackened, charred wood, he put it to one side. It was slow work. It was not that he was afraid of being burnt by the living embers he knew were in there. He wanted to be careful not to disturb them. They were the seed of the next fire. If he let them extinguish, he would have to go across to the cookhouse for a burning brand and that was not something he relished. Besides, the chance of getting it back alight to the barrack was slim in such weather.

After a few minutes, he felt a gentle warmth on his

hand. Kneeling down and putting his face close to the door, he peered into the stove. At the very rear, a thin wisp of smoke was eddying up from the ashes. He gently blew upon them. A small red glow shone momentarily. One by one, Ted positioned the fragments of charred wood delicately on top of the living embers. Like charcoal, they would soon catch.

Beside the stove was the fuel box. Ted lifted the lid to remove some dry wood to place in the stove once the fire got going. Except for a few strips of kindling and some pieces of bark, the box was empty. Whoever had been on stove duty the evening before had forgotten to fill it in readiness for the morning. There was nothing for it. He would have to brave the blizzard and fetch some wood from the stash stored under the barrack where it was comparatively dry.

Time was of the essence. The charred wood was beginning to burn. Ted put the bark and kindling on the embers then made for the barrack door. As he reached it, it opened and a flurry of dense heavy snowflakes blew in to scatter on the floor like glossy confetti.

'Where're you going?' asked Bob, materializing out of the storm.

'Wood,' Ted replied enigmatically.

Putting down a leather bucket of compacted snow, Bob said, 'I'll give you a hand.'

The wind was biting. The snow struck against their chests. The hole where Bob had excavated the contents of his bucket was already filling. They made their way to the leeward side of the barrack where the snow had not blocked access to the space between the floor of the barrack and the ground.

'I'll go in, throw some out to you,' Ted said through pursed lips. He knew that if he opened his mouth too wide, the snow would drive in as if to smother him: and he also knew the air was cold enough to injure his lungs and even crack the enamel on his teeth.

Under the barrack, it was dark. On the far side a wall of snow cut out what daylight was able to filter through the blizzard. Ted paused a moment to let his eyes adjust to the gloom then, on hands and knees, he crawled to the woodpile which he could just make out. Mercifully, the wood was dry. As quickly as he could, he selected smaller pieces that would ignite easily and started tossing these back towards Bob, whose legs he could see silhouetted against the grey light outside.

Tugging a larger log free of the pile, a movement behind it caught Ted's eye. For a moment, he thought it might be a rat or one of the feral cats that roamed through the camp hunting them. Not wanting to be bitten, he clapped his hands.

A spectral face, white as flour with sunken eyes and colourless lips appeared over the top of the wood pile. A pallid hand rose in a sort of salute. Both seemed disembodied, hanging in the air.

Ted let out a muted scream and started frantically scrabbling away, clouting his head on the floor joists of the barrack above him. The face moved and started to follow him, drifting jerkily through the semi-darkness. Ted backed up against one of the brick pillars upon which the barrack was built. His retreat was cut off. A hand hit his shoulder. He jumped and grunted with fear.

'What is it?'

It was Bob's hand.

'I–I don't know!' Ted stuttered. 'Look …'

The face seemed to be hovering in the half-light, pleading to them with imploring eyes. Two hands appeared and spread apart beseechingly. The mouth opened and spoke, the sounds guttural, rasping and incomprehensible.

'What's it saying?' Bob wondered aloud, his eyes wide with fright.

'He's a Czarist,' a voice said behind them, only just discernible over the hiss of the blizzard. Ted glanced over his shoulder. Pankhurst, hunched in a heavy overcoat with the collar turned up, was crouching behind them, his hair speckled with huge snowflakes. 'Let's get him inside.'

Ted and Bob, their fear dissipated, edged forwards and took the man's hands. They were as icy as a corpse's and grimed with dirt. With difficulty, for he was stiff from the cold, they half-dragged him to the edge of the barrack where Pankhurst and Ted hoisted him to his feet. He could not stand so they carried him between them while Bob collected up the firewood.

Inside Hut 7, the prisoners were now awake, though many had stayed in their bunks for warmth, awaiting the arrival of the morning porridge and mug of tea. When they saw the newcomer, they gathered around him.

'He's a Russian,' Pankhurst announced. 'The Germans brought in some Russian prisoners at nightfall. Just turned them loose in the compound. Most found their way to temporary quarters in Hut 16. This one must've got lost and spent the night under our billet.'

'Poor blighter!' someone exclaimed.

As soon as they had helped the Russian to a bench close to the stove, Ted paid his immediate attention to the fire which, though small, had taken hold. He strategically added more wood, which quickly flared. Smoke started to waft out of the stove door and seep from the crack in the chimney to form a warm, blue cloud up in the rafters. When he turned back to face the Russian, he was shocked.

What Ted had assumed was a man was in fact a teenage boy barely older than himself. His trousers, several sizes too big for him and held in place by a makeshift belt of cord, were in tatters while his torso was covered in nothing but a thick, coarse woollen vest. Tugged tight around his head and shoulders was what looked like a shawl but were the remnants of an army blanket. He wore no boots or shoes, his feet bound in strips from the same blanket, tied above his knees to stop them unravelling.

'Dear God in Heaven!' exclaimed Archy Ross, a blunt Suffolk fisherman. 'Is this the best the Czar of All the Russias can do? He's nowt but cannon fodder. Just some poor peasant dragged in to make up the numbers.'

'On my guvnor's farm,' remarked Pete Dodd, in a musical Welsh lilt, 'we dressed our scarecrows better than that.'

'Best get his clothes off,' Pankhurst said. 'We've got to get him dry and warm. Now, lads, let's have some blankets smartish. And we'll have to have a whip-round for some togs for him. Ted,' he continued, 'you help me.'

The Russian offered no resistance as Ted removed the blanket from his head and shoulders. He just stared absent-mindedly at the flames that were beginning to flicker and dance in the stove, his face set in a kind of far-away smile.

'He's a bit …' Ted searched for the right word '… dreamy.'

'He's got hypothermia,' Pankhurst said. 'His body's so cold it's started to close his brain down. Another hour at most and he'd have frozen to death.'

The Russian's hair was cut short and matted with filth, his neck as grimy as if he had worked soot into it. Despite being so cold, he smelt mustily of sour cheese and stale sweat. When Pankhurst removed his woollen vest, he made no effort to raise his arms to help and Ted had to hold them up, lowering them after the garment was off. Bare to the waist, the young man's skin looked almost translucent, tinged a faint blue. Every vein seemed as if it had been drawn in dark-blue ink with a fine pen. His ribs stood out, reminding Ted of the skeletal frame of an old rowing boat that had been stuck for years in the mud of Clovelly harbour. Like his neck, his body was filthy.

'If he's so cold,' Ted wondered aloud, reaching for the knotted cord tied around the Russian's waist, 'why isn't he shivering?'

'He's too far gone for that,' Pankhurst said. 'Shivering is a way the body has of creating heat out of energy. This poor soul's got no energy left. I think,' he continued, looking at Ted fumbling with the knot in the cord, 'we'll leave his trousers on for now. I daren't think what state he's in. But do his feet. We need to warm his extremities.'

Squatting in front of the Russian, Ted started to unravel the cloth bindings from his right leg. Being closer to the stove than the rest of him, the material was beginning to thaw out and grow damp.

'Here,' Pankhurst said, leaning over and handing Ted a clasp-knife. 'Cut them off. He's not going to need them again.'

Working from his ankle, Ted slipped the blade under the material and began gently cutting. The bindings fell away to reveal a thick woollen sock underneath. When the strips of cloth were all removed, he lifted the Russian's leg on to his thigh and very slowly began to peel the sock downwards, easing it round the heel. Like his torso, his leg was pale with the veins prominent under the skin. It felt clammy to the touch.

'Go easy,' cautioned Pankhurst.

The other prisoners gathered round, watching. One put his hand on the Russian's shoulder and said, 'You'll be all right, matey,' yet the Russian showed no sign of recognition. He just kept staring at the stove close to which Pete Dodd held two blankets, warming them.

Finally, Ted reached the end of the Russian's foot and slid the sock free. The toes were as black as one of the pieces of charred wood in the fire, the nails peeling upwards from the flesh.

'Frozen solid,' a voice said quietly.

Ted took hold of the Russian's leg to lower it to the floor. As he did so, he brushed the big toe against the side of his thigh. The toe broke off, fell to the floor and rolled away. Ted stared at it until it came to rest against one of the legs of the stove: then he passed out.

By midday, the young Russian soldier was dead.

PART THREE

APRIL 1917

Early in April, the weather suddenly warmed. Overnight, the last vestiges of snow disappeared and the thin glazing of ice around the edge of the lake melted. Within days, the mauve and orange spears of crocus flowers were pushing through the soil in the lawn of the German officers' beer garden, close by their accommodation building. Outside the perimeter fence, the trees became hazed with green as their buds began to burst.

After months of being pent-up in their barracks, the prisoners spent as much time as possible in the open air. Those who tended the vegetable plots set to digging and hoeing, fertilizing the soil with dung collected from the horses that delivered supplies. The theatrical club began planning its next production, Gilbert and Sullivan's *The Pirates of Penzance*. The occupants of each barrack spring-cleaned their quarters, repairing the ravages of winter as best they could.

A boost was given to this work by the *Kommandant* who was informed that the camp would be visited in late May by a party of Red Cross representatives. Made up of citizens from neutral countries not involved in the war, it was their task to ensure that the prisoners were being well-treated according to international law.

To put on a good show for them, the *Kommandant* ordered all the barracks to be painted with creosote, the barrack numbers touched up in white and the roofs re-tarred. Cartloads of gravel were delivered to bed down the pathways and the parade ground was lined by large stones painted white. He even provided five dozen mature black- and redcurrant bushes to be planted here and there to, as he put it in a speech to the prisoners at *Appell* one morning, 'make no starkness in the camp'.

When they were not busy about their chores, the prisoners indulged in any activity that took them out of their quarters. Pankhurst's classes in seamanship were held in the open air as were lessons in drawing, English grammar and spelling, history and geography.

Most of the prisoners formed into physical training exercise groups. The enforced idleness of winter had let them get out of condition. Now they could get their muscles back into shape. Dan Copley made a large vaulting horse while 'Goody' Goodenough organized an inter-barrack boxing contest. The cricket and bowls teams held practice sessions.

Yet the most common leisure pastime that involved everybody was universally known as treading the bounds.

The camp was contained by two parallel barbed-wire perimeter fences, each four metres high, between which ran a corridor two metres wide. Within this was a pathway along which the sentries patrolled. Inside the inner fence was another space of about three metres' width demarcated by a simple tripwire. The prisoners were forbidden to step into this area and up to the fence: to do so was to invite being shot by a sentry from one of the watchtowers erected every hundred metres along the fence.

However, the prisoners could approach as far as the tripwire, which was, in effect, the limit of their world. Just as caged animals do in a zoo, they often walked along it, creating a track way which encircled the entire camp. This track was referred to as the bounds.

One afternoon, Ted and Bob set off together to do a spin or two, as a full circuit of the camp was known. They had spent the morning in a navigation lesson, learning how to fix a position by the use of a three-arm protractor that Pankhurst had made out of wooden rulers and a circle of cardboard. The mathematics had been difficult to grasp and, by the time the lesson ended, they needed a spin to clear their heads of tangents and angles.

For the first few minutes, neither of them spoke. The sun warmed their shoulders and a light breeze ruffled their hair, cut short to combat head lice now spring had arrived.

'Have you thought,' Bob said, breaking their silence after they had passed two watchtowers, 'what it would be like out there?' He nodded in the direction of the wire and the woodland beyond.

'No. I try not to,' Ted answered, yet it was a lie. He had been increasingly thinking about what it was like on the other side of the wire.

'I mean,' Bob continued, 'what's Germany like? For example, do they have pubs? They don't play cricket so

what do they play? Do they have a town band …?'
He paused then added, 'I'm in our town band. Back
home. Trombone …'

They walked slowly on. Bob kicked at the earth. It
was dry. A small cloud of dust drifted up from the toe
of his boot. Several other prisoners, walking briskly for
exercise, passed them by.

'What're you going to do after …?' he ventured.

'After what?' Ted asked.

'After we get out of here. After the war. I mean, it
can't go on for ever.'

'It depends,' Ted replied thoughtfully, 'on who wins.'

Until that moment, neither of them had ever
considered the future. They lived, as all the prisoners did,
from day to day. There was no long term. No one could
see past the next meal, or the next *Appell*, or the next
theatrical show. It was a deliberate choice not to think
ahead. The future posed too many questions, created too
many hopes, reminded them too much of the past and
of how uncertain what was yet to be might be.

'We'll win, of course,' Bob rejoined.

'How can you be so sure?' Ted said. 'We don't know
what's going on. We don't get the news. For all we
know, the German army could be on the verge of
victory this very week.'

'That's defeatist talk,' Bob declared curtly.

'No,' Ted retorted. 'That's realist talk. I think we will
win,' he went on, 'but nothing's certain. You've got to
be ready for anything.'

'All right,' Bob said. 'If we win, what will you do?'

Ted thought for a moment. 'I'm still in the Navy,' he
replied. 'I suppose I'll go back to sea.'

'I won't,' Bob stated bluntly. 'I've had enough of that.'

Up ahead of them, a prisoner was standing quite still looking out towards the camp fence, his shins right up against the tripwire. He had his hands in his pockets.

'So what will you do?' Ted asked.

'I've been thinking,' Bob said. 'There's going to be great opportunities after the war. They'll need people in the factories, to replace all the men killed in the war. My town's got a lot of factories,' he added. 'I'm going to get me an apprenticeship in one of those factories, work hard, go to the institute and pass exams. One day, I'll be foreman ...'

Ted recognized the prisoner as they approached him. He was Liam Muldoon, an Ulsterman from Belfast who had been one of the crew of HMS *Nestor*.

'Will you just look at that, boys?' he asked, as Ted and Bob drew level with him. He spoke with a soft, rich, melodious Irish accent. 'Have you ever seen such beauty in all your life?'

Ted and Bob peered through the mesh of barbed wire. All there was to see was the line of trees a hundred metres into freedom.

'I can't see anything,' Bob remarked, giving Ted a glance. 'Just the woods.'

'Boys, boys!' Muldoon said, in a slightly chiding tone. 'Will you only see the big things in life? Mark my words, there's more to life than them. Look,' he continued, not for one moment shifting his eyes from the parallel fences, 'if someone shows you a grand painting, do you just stand back and say, "My! That's a fine picture you've got there, mister." Of course, you don't! You go up to it and you look at the detail. Down in the corner, under the hayrick, there's a tiny mouse. And he's as finely painted as the portrait of a king. And he's what makes the picture grand. The little things that all add up to make the greater beauty.'

At that moment, Ted saw what it was that had captivated Muldoon. In the corridor between the two fences, just to the side of the narrow pathway the guards had worn, was a small clump of emerald green leaves. From the centre, three or four slender white flower stalks were growing erect. One had opened into blossom, a tiny yellow star against the background of trodden earth, tall wooden poles and dull grey barbed wire.

'You've seen it, have you not, Ted?' Muldoon asked. His gaze was still fixed on the flower which shimmered in the breeze.

'Yes,' Ted confirmed. 'It's a primrose.'

'That's for sure,' Muldoon agreed. 'You know, boys, I know a place near Ballyronan, on the shores of Lough Neagh, where there's whole fields of them in the spring. Like a carpet made of butter, they are ...'

Ted and Bob carried on their spin. Just as they reached the next watchtower, some sixth sense − he could not tell what it was − made Ted glance back over his shoulder. Thirty metres along the fence, Muldoon was stepping slowly, deliberately over the tripwire. Ted froze. Words came to his mouth but he could not speak them. Bob walked on, not realizing Ted had stopped.

Muldoon was in no hurry. In five steps, he was up to the inner fence. Still, he was looking at the flower. Almost thoughtfully, as a man might reach out to stroke the cheek of a small child, Muldoon took his hands from his pockets, resting his right against one of the fence posts.

Bob, realizing Ted had stopped, turned round and saw Muldoon.

'Dear Lord!' he half-whispered. 'He's not going to …'

Muldoon put his left foot on the bottom strand of barbed wire and slowly lifted himself off the ground. His right foot tentatively felt for the next strand up.

From the watchtower above, Ted heard a guttural voice shout, '*Halt! Halt! Verschwinde! Runter vom Zaun!*'

Muldoon was oblivious. He slowly climbed higher up the inner fence. From over his head, Ted heard the metallic rattle of a rifle bolt opening and closing. It jarred him into action.

Running at full tilt towards Muldoon, his arms flailing to keep his balance, Ted screamed, 'Muldoon! No! Get down!'

Now five strands of barbed wire up, Muldoon paused for a moment. Ted reached the point on the path where Muldoon had been standing.

'Get down!' he yelled then, looking in the direction of the watchtower, he waved his arms about and bellowed, 'Don't shoot! Don't shoot!'

'*Nicht schiessen! Nicht schiessen!*' shouted another prisoner.

Two more sentries came running along the path between the perimeter fences, unslinging their rifles as they went.

Muldoon paid no attention whatsoever either to the guards or to Ted. He continued to climb up the fence at his own leisurely pace, reaching the top.

'Don't move!' Ted hollered. 'Muldoon! Keep still.'

'*Nicht bewegen!*' shouted one of the running guards.

Prisoners began to appear out of the barracks, drawn by the shouting. At first, they called to each other, asking what the ruckus was all about but, as they arrived upon the scene, they fell silent and stood back to watch.

Balancing on the top of the fence, Muldoon cautiously lifted his left leg over the top strand to avoid the material of his trousers being snagged on one of the barbs.

'Muldoon,' Ted said, no longer raising his voice, hoping that by talking in a normal tone he might somehow draw his attention. 'Don't risk it. Come on down. It's only a flower.'

For a moment, Muldoon paused and looked straight at Ted. He smiled but he did not speak. Instead, he started to raise his right leg.

A single shot rang out. Muldoon pitched backwards, his spine arched, his arms flung outwards like a man being crucified. His body went slack but did not fall. A second shot sounded. Muldoon's body quivered at the impact of the bullet, slumped and fell, the barbed wire ripping into his clothing and flesh, holding him suspended in mid-air.

Ted stared at him hanging limply from the top of the fence. Tears welled up in his eyes. He felt his throat harden. An arm went round his shoulder.

'Come along, Ted,' Pankhurst said quietly. 'There's nothing more to be done.'

Ted stepped resolutely forward, over the tripwire.

Muldoon's footsteps were plain to see in the untrodden, forbidden strip of earth. Placing his own boots in them, he walked to the fence. Muldoon's blood was dripping down the fence, from strand to strand to soak into the dry earth. The two guards came up, their rifles pointing at Ted.

At the fence, Ted knelt and, pressing his shoulder to the wire, he pushed his arm through. His fingers just reached the primrose. With his finger and thumb, he picked the single blossom then, standing up, turned his back on the fence, stepping towards the tripwire. The guards, seeing him retreat, lowered their rifles.

Just short of the tripwire, Ted stopped. Ahead of him, a large crowd of prisoners watched him in silence. Nearest to him was Pankhurst, his hand outstretched. Very slowly, Ted moved round to face the two German guards. Looking them straight in the eye, he dropped the yellow flower to the earth. Then, with all the deliberation he could muster, he ground it into the soil with his heel.

It was a week after Muldoon's funeral (with full military honours and all the prisoners attending) before Ted could bring himself to take another spin. He set out on several but, as he approached the place where Muldoon had climbed the wire, he had had to turn back. He blamed himself for not acting, for not running forward and grabbing him by the legs. Had there been two of them, he was sure the guards would not have opened fire. They would not have considered it a hair-brained escape but a bit of larking about, punishable by a week in solitary confinement rather than death.

Finally, he faced up to it, set off alone and reached the dreaded spot, where he halted. The Germans had raked the footprints out of the soil between the tripwire and the fence but there was still a darkish patch, which Ted knew contained Muldoon's blood. As for the primrose, the other buds had since opened and faded.

'Don't dwell on it,' a voice said with quiet sympathy as Ted stared at the barbed wire.

He turned to discover a soldier dressed in the remnants of a corporal's uniform standing behind him. He was short and wiry, with curly hair and a crown tattooed on his arm. Ted could not help noticing there was a nick out of one of his ears.

'It weren't Fritz what done that,' the soldier continued, in a rich Cockney accent. 'Beer bottle in the public bar of the Londoner's Arms, that was. Bit of a fighter, me. Before the war, see.' He laughed. 'Me name's Wilkie. Royal Artillery. Got took near Wipers, I did.'

'Ted Foley,' Ted answered, 'HMS *Nomad*. My ship was sunk at Jutland.'

'Good to know yer,' Wilkie said, shaking Ted's hand. 'Now look, chum,' he went on. 'What's done's done. Yer can't undone it. But –' he put his hand on Ted's arm and guided him on along the path – 'yer can do something else. Not just for yer dead shipmate. For King an' Country. For the war effort.'

'I've been thinking about that,' Ted said.

'An' what yer going to do? What're yer plans?'

'Escape,' Ted answered bluntly.

Since Muldoon's death, the idea had preyed upon his mind. He knew the chances of making it back to Britain were slim in the extreme but, at the very least, he believed, he had to do something. He could not just sit cooped up in Brandenburg, making the *Evelyn*, attending seamanship lessons hundreds of miles from the sea, acting in amateur dramatics and watching people get shot for wanting to pick a flower. After all, as Commander Stannard had reminded them all, it was their duty to escape.

'Escape!' Wilkie exclaimed. 'The king'll 'ave kittens first! No, that's not a good idea, chum.'

'If I were to escape,' Ted said, 'I'd be helping the war effort. The Germans would have to send out patrols to find me. As I travelled through Germany, I could note all I saw and report on it when I got back ...'

'*If* you got back, chum. If the Germans pick yer up with a notebook full of useful information, they'll shoot yer for a spy. No,' Wilkie continued, 'I've got a better idea. Less risk, more trouble for Fritz. An' I need a little gang of 'elpers. Yer game?'

'What is it?' Ted asked.

'In the next couple of weeks, we're all going to be made to work for Fritz. They ain't supposed to do it, because that's not right and it's against the law. Even wars 'as laws. But they don't care about that, see? So —'

'How do you know?' Ted interrupted.

'This ain't my first camp,' Wilkie explained. 'I was in two others. I've been a PoW for twenty-one months. As soon as spring come, they 'ad us out on the land. Diggin' potatoes, sowin' seeds, plantin' plants, cleanin' ditches. Some of the lads was made to work in an ammunition factory. Making the shells that was goin' to kill their mates. It was wrong, aidin' the enemy, whatever way yer look at it. Fritz shot the cartridges and ate the cabbages.'

'Couldn't they do anything?' Ted asked.

'Oh, they did!' Wilkie replied with a grin. 'They put too much explosive in some of the shells. You slip one of them into the breech and –' he snapped his fingers – 'Bang! Blow-back! One dead Fritz gun crew, one useless piece of artillery.' Two German sentries approached along the pathway between the fences. Wilkie fell silent. 'Around 'ere,' he carried on once they were out of earshot, 'there ain't no factories but there is farms. Yer can bet yer buttons they'll 'ave us labourin' in the fields. So we got to be prepared.'

'What do you want me to do?' Ted asked.

'What 'ut you in?'

'Hut 7.'

'Right! I ain't got a bloke in 7. 'Ere's what I want yer to do. I want yer to collect up razor blades. When the lads in yer 'ut are finished with a blade, I don't want 'em throwin' 'em out. Yer make sure you get 'em. And yer give 'em to me. See?'

Ted was puzzled and said, 'Razor blades are in short supply. They don't throw them away until they're really blunt. What use can they be?'

'All will be revealed,' Wilkie replied with a wink and, with that, he reached down, tore a weed growing at his feet out of the ground, gave a little wave with the leaves and walked off. 'See yer around, chum,' he said as, to Ted's amazement, he stuffed the plant in his pocket.

Four days later, Wilkie's prediction came true. After morning *Appell*, *Hauptmann* Vogel stood on the dais and addressed the assembly.

'Prisoners!' he began in a pompous voice. 'From today, you will work for Germany. As prisoners, you are a cost on the German people. We have to house you and feed you ...'

'You can send us home, if you like!' a voice called out from the midst of the lines of prisoners. The remark was met by guffaws of laughter and shouts of '*Still! Still!*' from the guards.

'... And so,' the *Hauptmann* went on when the laughter had died down, 'you will start to earn your keep.' He smiled expansively. 'But we Germans are a fair people. We do not expect you to work for nothing. All prisoners working will receive pay of five pfennigs per day. This may be spent as you wish purchasing items from a shop in the Parcels Office.'

'In other words,' someone in the row behind Ted muttered, 'we work for money we have to give back. That's rich, that is!'

'You will be divided into labour units,' Vogel continued. 'You will work hard. If you are lazy, you will be punished. Only sick men do not work. Each labour unit is twenty men. Arrange yourselves in units. You will go to your work in one hour.'

With that, the *Hauptmann* stepped down off the dais. The prisoners all began talking at once. The rumours that had been circulating in the camp were true: they were to be used as labour. Commander Stannard took Vogel's place on the platform.

'Gentleman,' he shouted. Instantly, all the prisoners

fell silent. 'You will all be aware that it is contrary to the conventions of war that prisoners be made to work for the enemy cause. However, we do not want German reprisals. Furthermore, the work may give us hitherto unforeseen opportunities …' He paused and briefly coughed.

Every prisoner understood the meaning of that clearing of his throat: it was his message to them all to use their work whenever possible, in even the tiniest of ways, to undermine the German war effort.

'… to earn a little money with which to purchase a few luxuries,' he went on, disguising his real intention from the Germans. 'I, for one, would love to have a fresh egg.' Commander Stannard changed his tone of voice. 'Huts are to arrange themselves in work units. All units to parade here in forty-five minutes. Carry on.'

'They're only paying us to make it look good,' Bob remarked as he and Ted headed back to their hut. 'That way they can't say we're slave labour. Slaves don't get a wage.'

Ted did not reply. He was already planning. That payment, no matter how tiny, would be the start of his savings, his escape fund.

Outside his barrack, Wilkie was waiting for Ted.

'Ted,' he said, 'don't get chose for a unit with yer 'ut-mates. Yer come with me.'

Following Wilkie, Ted entered the ablutions building. They walked past the long line of lavatory cubicles to the end where there was a concrete floor from which pipes rose up to a row of brass shower nozzles. Gathered there was a group of prisoners.

'Yer all 'eard what the Commander said,' Wilkie

addressed them. 'Only with us, they ain't unforeseen opportoon-ities, are they, lads?' A chuckle went round the group. 'Now we got our chance to fight back a bit. Everybody ready?'

A few nodded in reply.

'What are we going to do?' Ted asked. 'We've no weapons …'

He was pleased to be included as a member of this gang but he had no idea what his role would be, apart from collecting useless razor blades, nor how they could effectively strike back at the Germans.

'What are we goin' to do?' Wilkie echoed. He looked round the group who were all smirking conspiratorially. ''E don't know, do 'e? Shall we …?'

''E's one of us. Give 'im a gander,' someone suggested.

Two of the prisoners stepped forward and made a cradle with their hands.

'Step in 'ere, sunshine,' one of them ordered Ted. 'We're goin' to give you a bunk up.'

With the agility of a circus acrobat, Wilkie swung himself up on the shower pipe and pushed at a section of the flat ceiling. A disguised trap door opened over his head and he raised himself into it. Ted was lifted up and Wilkie, stretching down, took hold of his arms until he had a footing on the pipe.

'Join me in my laborat'ry,' Wilkie invited him.

Ted hoisted himself into the roof space. It was dark, with only a few tiny chinks of light leaking in through cracks in the eaves.

'Yer say we got no weapons,' Wilkie said, keeping his voice down to a loud whisper, 'but we got thousands of 'em. Follow me but make sure yer only step on the

75

rafters. We don't want a tell-tale 'ole in the ceiling of the bogs below, do we?'

Carefully, Ted followed Wilkie down the attic. The pitch of the roof was so low they could only move crouched up. At the end, standing on planks running across the rafters, were several dozen small cages with tight wire mesh fronts.

'Fritz never looks up 'ere,' Wilkie remarked.

'What are they?' Ted asked.

'Come 'ere,' Wilkie said, sliding the top off one of the cages. ''Ave a shuftie in this one.'

Ted peered into the box. Much to his consternation, upon a layer of fresh green leaves, was a seething tangle of small, pale yellow caterpillars with black spots on each segment of their bodies.

'Don't get it, do yer?' Wilkie said. 'Never mind, yer will. Now give us an 'and.' He pulled a cardboard Red Cross parcel carton out from behind the cages. It was full of empty matchboxes. 'We been savin' these. Put about two dozen caterpillars in each one. Go easy. It's best to pick up a leaf and shake 'em in. Don't try pickin' 'em up. We don't want to 'urt the little darlin's.'

'How have you bred them?' Ted asked. It seemed inconceivable that someone could raise thousands of caterpillars in a dark attic.

'Easy!' Wilkie replied. 'In the winter, I did a tour of all the 'uts in the camp. Looked in cracks and crevices, found me over forty chriss-liss-iss. They like to winter over in buildings. Kept 'em warm, looked after 'em. Nurtured 'em like they was me own kids. Two weeks ago, when the days got warm, they 'atched into butterflies. I picked some flowers then put 'em all together in the cages. They did what the birds an' the bees do, laid their eggs an' – Bingo!'

'But how did you know what to feed them on?'

Wilkie touched his nose with his finger and said, 'That's the trick.'

When twenty boxes were filled, Ted and Wilkie climbed down from the roof and handed them round.

'Don't go givin' 'em names,' Wilkie advised, with a twinkle in his eyes. 'They ain't pets. They're our secret weapon.'

'What are they for?' Ted wanted to know. He was, to put it mildly, curious as to how they could fight Germany with a matchbox full of caterpillars.

'You'll see,' Wilkie replied.

An hour later, the prisoners were assembled on the parade ground in units of twenty. A column of German soldiers marched in through the main camp gate, five assigned to each unit. The *Kommandant* addressed the prisoners. His message was curt and succinct.

'From now on, six days a week, you will work for Germany. You will not escape. The soldiers with you have orders to shoot. No warning.'

With that stark message ringing in their ears, and the memory of Muldoon's fate in their minds, the prisoners were marched out of the camp for the first time since they had been captured.

Ted's unit, with half a dozen others, was sent to a farm about an hour's march from the camp. Between the bank of the River Havel and a railway line, equidistant from the villages of Fohrde and Tieckow, the farmhouse was an ancient building surrounded by a few barns and animal pens.

The remains of a mill stood on the river bank by a jetty that had perhaps once been used to land feed for the animals or to take produce away to market by river barge. It had clearly fallen into disuse with the war and was in some state of disrepair. Where the barges might have once moored there was now only a small and somewhat decrepit boat with a single mast tied up to a rusting bollard.

The farm was predominantly arable with about ten acres set aside for the grazing of the plough-horses and the raising of pigs.

On arrival, the work units were lined up before a large barn to be allotted their tasks. Just as Wilkie had assumed, they were to help with the spring planting and sowing. One by one, the units were taken into the barn to collect tools and either small sacks of seeds or shallow wooden trays of seedlings. Ted's team were given seeds but, once outside, Wilkie had a word with one of the seedling units and they all surreptitiously swapped equipment.

'Got yer little friends?' he asked Ted as they made their way under guard to a newly tilled field.

'Friends?' Ted replied.

'Yer know.' Wilkie nodded towards his pocket. 'Yer little wriggly pals.'

'Yes,' Ted said and he reached into his pocket.

'Don't bring 'em out!' Wilkie hissed.

At the field, the twenty men lined up. One of the German guards, an elderly man with a pronounced limp, handed Wilkie, who had appointed himself unit leader, a piece of paper. Upon it was written:

> *Soljers lin up and pland the babby plands*
> *in lins 40 cms appartt evry 40 cms. Lins*
> *must bee strayt. No bens.*

After working out the spelling, he read the instructions and the unit spread out along the field edge. Each man had a tray of seedlings and a wooden dibber.

'Right, lads,' Wilkie addressed them before they began. 'Yer know what to do. God save the King!'

The guards positioned themselves around the field. There were only five of them. Three were too old for active service while the other two had been in the fighting at the front and were too badly wounded to return.

'Look at 'em,' Wilkie remarked as he started planting out the seedlings. 'Talk about old and infirm. If we was to scarper, not one of 'em could run as fast as us and as for shoot without warning ... That barn'd be safe at twenty paces.'

'Shows the state of the nation, though, dunnit?' observed one of the other prisoners, a soldier with a short crop of ginger hair and a livid scar on his neck. 'All the fit blokes are off at the front. No one left at 'ome except ol' codgers and cripples. I reckon the war'll not last much longer. They'll run out of men before they run out of bullets.'

'Don't count on it, Ginge,' Wilkie advised. 'The same could apply to us.'

'Are these cabbages?' Ted enquired, kneeling on the ground and making a hole with his dibber.

'Spot on!' Wilkie exclaimed with obvious pleasure.

For fifteen minutes, the men worked in a line out into the field. The earth soiled their trousers and boots and got under their fingernails. Here and there, gobbets of pig dung had been spread across the field for fertilizer. As the sun warmed the ground, it began to smell sweet and sickly. No one talked. They just edged along, pushing their seedling trays in front of them, dibbing a little hole, putting a seedling in it, firming down the roots and moving on. It was back-breaking work. Every so often, Wilkie would stand up to ease his muscles and order someone to move over a bit to keep the rows more or less in straight lines.

'Just as I thought,' Wilkie remarked at length, glancing round the field. The guards were not moving with the prisoners but holding station on the edge of the field. He turned to Ginge working the row next to him. 'Time to open fire,' he said. 'Pass it on.'

'What do you mean?' Ted asked, somewhat alarmed. He was not so sure about the inability of the sentries to shoot accurately. The old men might miss a barn but the two younger ones had had battlefield experience.

'Don't fret, Ted,' Wilkie reassured him. 'We ain't firing bullets. Take out yer little chums and put them in the tray.' He took his own matchbox from his pocket and placed it next to his unplanted seedlings. Carefully, he opened the box. The caterpillars were active, creeping over each other and trying to climb free. 'Lovely!' he said, with a quiet satisfaction. 'Look at 'em.

'Ungry as lions.' He nudged them back in and slid the box shut.

'What exactly are they?' Ted enquired.

'They are caterpillars,' Wilkie replied, stating the obvious. '*Exactly*,' he went on, chorusing Ted, 'they are the caterpillars of the large white butterfly, otherwise known as the cabbage white. Common as shells on the seashore. See 'em everywhere. Soon to be a feature of the cabbage fields of Germany.'

For a moment, Ted was speechless.

'You mean …' he started.

'That's right,' Wilkie said. 'See, Fritz eats pickled cabbages. Love 'em, 'e do. *Sauerkraut*, 'e calls it. Basic nosh for your average German.' His voice grew somewhat less humorous. 'Now, cabbage goes rotten quickly after picking but pickled, it lasts for months. That makes it an ideal food for soldiers. Now you get it?'

Ted nodded.

'You put one caterpillar on every sixth seedling,' Wilkie continued. 'In an hour or two, they'll have munched it to a stalk and moved on to the next one. They can smell a cabbage better than a blood-'ound smells blood. Couple of days and the field's done for. No *sauerkraut* for Fritz.'

'An' no reprisal on us,' Ginge added. 'Act of nature.'

When the next seedling was firmly in the ground, Ted checked the guards were not looking then, carefully, so as not to harm any of the contents, he slid his matchbox open until there was just a crack at the end. Shaking it gently, a caterpillar fell on to the palm of his hand. He looked at it. It seemed impossible that such a tiny creature could wreak such damage. It started to walk over his skin. It was so small and insignificant, he could hardly feel its tiny feet and suckers.

Placing his hand against one of the seedling's leaves, he watched as the caterpillar reached the edge, paused to test the way ahead, decided it was safe – or edible – and stepped on to the plant. Ted moved on, an intense feeling of pleasure warming his soul as much as the sun was warming his back. It seemed almost nothing but he had, in a tiny and curious fashion, at last the chance to strike back at the enemy.

At one o'clock, the prisoners were ordered to stop work for an hour. They were herded together in the barn where a barrel of water and some enamel mugs were provided. Each unit was issued with three loaves of dense black bread, a kilo of hard cheese and two jars of what looked to Ted like pale reddish string surrounded by a maroon-tinged liquid.

'*Sauerkraut*,' Wilkie said, dipping his fingers in one of the jars. 'This is what Fritz ain't gettin' with 'is turkey next Christmas. 'Ere,' he added, holding a strand out for Ted, 'try a bit.'

Ted took it and sucked it into his mouth. It had a sharp, unpleasant taste yet it was, to his surprise, as crisp as a new-cut leaf.

'It's sour,' he remarked, after swallowing half a mug of water to rinse his mouth out.

'That's right,' Wilkie replied. '*Sauerkraut*. Sour cabbage. It's what it means.'

The sun was hot and high as they marched back to the field with new trays of seedlings. Walking along the rows they had planted in the morning, Ted tried to see the caterpillars but he could not. Furthermore, he could not see one seedling that showed even the least sign of having been eaten by tiny insect jaws.

'It's not working,' he said to Wilkie, a little despondently.

'Give 'em time,' Wilkie answered.

By six o'clock, all the seedlings were planted and all the caterpillars deployed. The unit had covered about a third of the field. The guards called the prisoners in to muster at the barn for the march back to the camp.

'Not a bad day's slog,' Wilkie commented with a wry smile as they collected the empty trays and began to trudge towards the farm.

Walking along the rows of seedlings, Ted purposely dropped his dibber. Stopping to pick it up, he quickly surveyed the young cabbage plants around him. One was eaten down to the stem, a caterpillar making its way unerringly across the rich brown, damp soil for the next.

'Shame they don't pay us by the seedlin',' Wilkie commented as Ted stood up. 'Another week an' this field'll need completely replantin'.'

At the farmyard, all tools were handed in and accounted for by the farmer. This done, the prisoners formed ranks and set off, four abreast, for the camp.

'Gives you a fair appetite, that farm work,' Ginge remarked as they crossed the railway line and headed down a cart track. He winked at Ted, checked the guards were nowhere near and half opened his coat. Hanging from a piece of twine suspended round his neck were two fat hens, swinging by their legs in time to his footsteps. Wilkie, walking next to him, took his hands out of his pockets. In each were two fresh eggs.

'Yer know 'ow to make a German om'lette?' Wilkie asked Ted.

Ted shook his head.

'First, yer steal two German eggs,' Wilkie replied and the other prisoners laughed.

'But how did you …?' Ted began.

'Charmed 'em off the trees,' Wilkie said.

The sun was setting by the time they reached the main camp gate. There, they were paraded, counted and dismissed.

'This is yours,' Wilkie said, handing Ted one of the eggs as he started off in the direction of Hut 7. 'Yer share of the spoils of war. Just don't eat it in front of that Commander Stannard.'

After thanking Wilkie for the egg, Ted said, 'Can I ask you something?' It was a question that had been burning in him for days.

'Ask away, chum,' Wilkie replied.

'What are the razor blades for?'

'Pigs,' Wilkie replied, enigmatically.

'Pigs?' Ted repeated.

'Pigs on farms eat swill,' Wilkie went on to explain. 'Leftovers, carrot tops, potato peelin's, hedge trimmin's, stale bread. Slop. Anything. The farms round 'ere 'ave been collectin' the garbage from the camp for some time. I guessed it was for feedin' to pigs …'

'I still don't understand,' Ted said.

'We break up the razor blades an' drop 'em in the slop. They might not be sharp enough to shave yer chin, but they are to slice open a pig's belly – if 'e swallers it. Now yer average German's no fool. 'E knows we put the razor blades – an' anything else sharp – in the slop. So, at first, they had a couple of privates detailed to go through the swill with their fingers. They didn't like that. Mucky work! An' they could get a nasty cut. Now, the slop's just chucked. The Germans can't risk it. Pigs grow thin, bacon's stringy an' got no fat on it. Everyone's unhappy. In Germany, anyway. Caught me drift?'

It was late. The final *Appell* had been called and the guards had done their rounds, locking the prisoners into their barracks for the night. Not long after the work units returned to camp, it had rained heavily. Now, the overcast sky filled with gloomy storm clouds, the twilight had quickly become darkness.

The oil lamp cast a warm, flickering glow over the tables in the barrack. From its glass chimney, it gave off a thin, sooty plume of smoke and a faint smell of paraffin. At one end of the table by the stove, two soldiers played draughts while, at the other end, Dan Copley concentrated on carving a stick, the flakes of wood scattered on the floor round his feet.

'I hope you're going to pick them up,' someone remarked in the semi-darkness. 'Come morning, I don't want splinters in my feet.'

'It's a soft wood,' Dan replied quietly. 'Still full of sap. No danger to your delicate skin.'

'What're you whittling at anyway?' asked one of the draughts players, looking up briefly from the game.

Dan made no attempt at a reply. Not taking his eye off his task, he carefully ran the blade of his knife along the stick, peeling off another sliver of white wood.

Ted's mind was getting numb but he was determined not to surrender to the difficulty of what he had set himself. Opening the book for the third time that evening, he glanced at the label pasted inside it. It was headed *British Prisoner of War Book Scheme (Educational)*. He turned the page. The title leaf read: *New Pocket Dictionary – German & English (Both Parts) – Containing All Words Requisite For Home Use And For Travel – by Dr F. E. Feller.*

At random, he moved his finger halfway along the book to arrive in the *M* section. Taking a deep breath, as if he were about to dive into icy water, he began to run his eye at random over the page.

'Match (safety) is *Sicherheitszündholz*,' he muttered to himself. 'Medicine is *Arznei*. Memento is *Erinnerung*.'

He stopped in despair. He was, he was certain, never going to get a grip on the German language. And yet, no sooner had this occurred to him than he saw words that were vaguely familiar. *Mild* meant mellow and *Fleisch* meant meat or flesh. A mat was *Matte* and a mechanic was a *Mechaniker*. Encouraged, he tried a few more pages then turned to the back of the book where there was a list of common phrases. He was about to start upon them when Bob came up to the table.

'What're you doing?' he asked, leaning over Ted's shoulder.

'Reading,' Ted answered non-committally.

'Reading what?' Bob went on. Before Ted could stop him, he had snatched the book up and was looking at it. 'It's Fritz!' he exclaimed. 'You're learning Fritz.'

'I'm just looking at it,' Ted defended himself.

'*Phrases of Use in a Hotel*,' Bob read aloud, sitting down on the bench beside Ted. '*Take my luggage to the station, please*.' He licked his finger and flicked the page over. '*I want to change some English money*. Not a lot of use that. Not in Brandenburg.'

'I'm just reading it for something to do,' Ted admitted evasively.

'What's the point?' Bob said. He turned back a page. '*Can you recommend a good boarding house to me?*' he read. 'I certainly can. Brandenburg PoW Camp. Cosy quarters, congenial fellow guests, secure accommodation …'

'You don't have to take the mickey,' Ted said curtly, snatching the book back and closing it.

'I didn't mean any harm,' Bob apologized.

'That's all right,' Ted replied. 'I'm turning in.'

He went down the barrack to his tier of bunks and climbed up. The draughts players finished their game. Copley put away his clasp-knife and blew out the oil lamp. All around were the sounds of men settling down to sleep, the straw in their palliasses rustling, the wooden frames of the bunks creaking. In a few minutes, Ted knew, he would hear the first tentative snores and yet, in his mind, he could hear himself above all the other sounds. *Von welchem Bahnsteig geht der Zug nach Berlin ab?* the voice in his head said. *From which platform does the train for Berlin go?*

PART FOUR

JUNE 1917

The weeks passed by. Every Saturday, after the work parties had all returned to the camp, there was a pay parade organized by *Feldwebel* Diepgen, one of the German administration office staff.

An ugly, thickset man with an almost neanderthal face, the *Feldwebel* was both feared and detested by the prisoners. He was a martinet, cruel and vicious and unpredictable. Sometimes, he would smile and be almost pleasant, in the way that a recently fed fox might be to a rabbit. At other times, for no apparent reason, he would lash out, his fist bunched. No prisoner dare strike him back. They just took it and harboured the dream that, one day, when the war was over and Britain and her allies were victorious, they would get their revenge on him.

Feldwebel Diepgen stood at the end of a long desk on the stage in Hut 16. Two German clerks were seated behind it, one with a heavy ledger and the other with a small steel strongbox full of low-denomination banknotes. One by one, the ledger clerk called the prisoners up to collect their week's wages. The second clerk counted out the sum due and folded it into a small brown envelope. Diepgen oversaw the whole operation, watching the Germans as closely as the prisoners.

'Like prize-giving at school,' Bob said as he and Ted waited in line on the first pay day in June. 'Mind you,' he went on, 'not that I ever won one. What'll you spend it on in the Parcels Office shop?'

'Nothing I want in there,' Ted answered. 'They only sell tobacco, cigarette papers and matches.'

'And photos,' Bob added.

'Postcards of the *Rathaus* in Brandenburg and the town square. Who wants that?'

'I'm collecting them,' Bob admitted. 'When we get free, I'll have them as souvenirs to remind me …'

'I don't want any souvenirs of this place,' Ted said vehemently.

'Not to show your mum, your dad, your friends? They'd like to know where you were.'

'I don't want them to know.' Ted looked down at his hands with dirt ingrained under his nails, at his trousers soiled at the knees with earth, at his boots covered with caked mud and pig dung. 'I'm not proud to be here. To be a labourer in the enemy's fields.'

'You can't escape the fact that you were a prisoner.'

'No,' Ted answered quietly, 'not the fact.'

The clerk called out his number and Ted climbed the steps to the desk. As he received his meagre pay of three ten-pfennig notes for six days' work, *Feldwebel* Diepgen stared at him. Ted felt the hairs on his neck prickle.

'Do you not say thank you?' the German asked in a

sneering voice as Ted accepted the money. 'The German people give you pay and you do not give thanks?'

Ted knew it was best either to say thank you or smile self-deprecatingly and walk off yet he could not bring himself to do either.

'I've earned it,' he replied sullenly.

For a moment, the *Feldwebel* made no comment. Then, with the dexterity of a snake, his hand lashed out. His fingers gripped the collar of Ted's coat, throwing him off-balance.

'You are ungrateful,' the *Feldwebel* screamed, pulling Ted around the desk, painfully barking his hip on the corner. 'You do not earn this money. You earn your keep. You work to grow the food you eat.'

A picture of Wilkie's caterpillars chewing their way through a cabbage seedling sprang immediately into Ted's mind. If that were true, he thought, they were all in for a meagre winter that year.

'I don't eat *sauerkraut*,' Ted declared loudly, so everyone could hear.

Feldwebel Diepgen stared at him. Ted stared back. The prisoners watched.

'You don't eat *sauerkraut*,' the German repeated, enunciating each word slowly. His eyes narrowed and Ted prepared himself for the punch he expected to follow. Instead, the *Feldwebel* let go of him. Ted stepped away and began to descend the steps of the stage. The moment Ted turned around, the German slammed both his fists into the small of his back. The double blow winded him and he let go of the three banknotes, which fluttered to the floor. A second blow projected him forwards. Ted fell heavily down the steps, ending up spread-eagled on the floorboards, gasping for breath. Pankhurst came forward to help him up.

'Leave him!' *Feldwebel* Diepgen commanded but Pankhurst ignored him. Several other prisoners, led by Wilkie, positioned themselves between Ted and the stage.

'Want to make somethin' of it?' Wilkie asked the *Feldwebel* in an offhand fashion.

Feldwebel Diepgen looked down and, after a pause, said, 'This is why you are losing the war. You are sending boys to do a man's work.'

'That's because our boys can do a man's job,' Wilkie answered, coolly, his eyes not shifting from the *Feldwebel*'s. 'In England, women work as pay clerks.'

For a moment, it looked as if the *Feldwebel* was going to explode with rage. His lips drew into a thin colourless line and he gripped the side of the desk, his fingers white and quivering. Yet he knew he was beaten. Turning on his heel, he snapped an order to the two clerks and marched out of the building, the prisoners moving aside to let him pass. Ted, catching his breath, collected his pfennigs from the floor.

When he left Hut 16, Ted did not join the queue outside the shop in the Parcels Office but returned to his barrack. Apart from a few prisoners sitting on the steps smoking and chatting in the last of the sunlight, Ted was on his own. Going to his tier of bunks, he checked no one was watching him, then, with a thick darning needle he kept inserted in the hem of his palliasse, he gently prised a knot of wood out of one of the uprights nearest to the wall to reveal a small cavity. It had taken him over a fortnight to hollow it out, working at night after everyone else was asleep.

Rolling the three banknotes into a tiny, tight cylinder, he slid them into the cavity, easing them in alongside those he had already earned.

'You don't need to do that.'

Ted jumped and turned round sharply. Standing watching him was Bob.

'You can't think much of your mates,' Bob continued, 'if you think someone's going to steal your money.'

'I'm not hiding it from you,' Ted justified himself. 'I'm hiding it so the Germans – so *Feldwebel* Diepgen – can't find it.'

'Even he's not going to nick it,' Bob rejoined. 'Thirty pfennigs is not exactly a king's ransom.'

'It's not thirty pfennigs,' Ted admitted. 'It's one hundred and fifty.'

Bob stared at him and said, 'That's everything we've been paid in five weeks. Haven't you spent any of it?'

'No,' Ted replied.

'There's no point saving it. It's not as if you could go into Brandenburg town, to the shops. You can't buy anything big with it.'

'Yes, there is,' Ted answered, but he did not elaborate on it.

'Like what?' Bob asked, a little sarcastically.

'You remember what Commander Stannard told us in his welcome speech?' Ted said.

'What about?'

'About needing maps, money,' Ted replied.

For a moment, Bob failed to grasp what Ted was implying: then the truth dawned on him.

'You mean ...' he began, but the enormity of what he thought Ted was talking about took his words away.

'That's right,' Ted assured him. 'This is my escape fund.'

'You can't mean it!' Bob exclaimed, his power of speech returning. 'We're hundreds of miles inside Germany. We're over the sea. This isn't like being in ...' He searched for a place nearer to home, '... Scotland.' He looked around for someone to come to his aid, support his argument, but there was no one else in the barrack. 'You've got no disguise. You can't escape looking like a Roman soldier or a pirate from Penzance.'

'I don't need a disguise,' Ted replied, his voice level and calm. 'Germans look just like us. I mean, I'm not Chinese or African or something.'

'You don't speak German,' Bob said, searching for another reason to dissuade Ted. 'Unless –' his voice took on a wheedling tone – ' "How much is a room in your hotel, please?" or "My elephant has chilblains and needs a hot cognac." '

'I do,' Ted replied, defensively. 'And not that rubbish, either.'

'Like what, for example?'

'Like *Guten Morgen* means Good morning. *Wie geht es Ihnen?* means How are you? *Bitte* means please. *Danke* means thank you.'

'And,' Bob warned ominously, '*Nicht schiessen.* Those could be the last words you utter.'

'You think that's not occurred to me?'

'Remember Muldoon,' Bob went on, believing he might at last be making some headway in the argument.

Ted pressed home the knot of wood that covered the cavity and said, 'There's not a day goes by when I don't remember him.'

'Do you have a plan?' Bob asked, trying another tack.

'Not yet,' Ted confessed. 'I've got to be ready before I decide how.'

After running his hand over the knot in the wood to make sure it was flush with the surface, Ted rubbed his palm on the floor and smeared a little dust over it. Even close inspection showed no sign of the cavity.

'That'll take a while,' Bob said, the relief obvious in his voice.

'Not as long as you might think,' Ted rejoined, nodding in the direction of the door.

Once outside, halfway along the barrack wall, Ted stopped and knelt down, pretending to tie his shoelace, all the time looking around to ensure no one was watching. Then, pulling Bob after him, he ducked into the space under the building.

'I got the idea just after we found the Russian soldier,' Ted said as they scrambled across the dry earth. 'The Germans seldom look under the huts and yet they would never be surprised at seeing someone come under here to get wood.' He stopped by one of the brick pillars. Reaching out, he set about carefully working a loose brick, moving it very gently to and fro. 'You see,' he went on as he eased the brick out, 'I guessed the pillars are hollow and ...'

The brick came away. Ted placed it on the ground and, reaching into the dark hole, removed a small tin box. On the lid was a torn and faded paper label that read *Jacob's Cream Crackers*. Prising the lid off, Ted showed Bob the contents – four small bars of Cadbury's chocolate, a tin of strawberry jam and two packets wrapped in greaseproof paper and tied with string.

'Where did you …?' Bob began.

'I've been saving my Red Cross parcels,' Ted replied, 'and swapping the tobacco in them with some of the others.'

'What're in the packages?' Bob wanted to know.

'One contains eight Tate & Lyle sugar cubes and the other three ship's biscuits. There's more.'

Ted thrust his arm into the hole in the pillar to produce two small hessian sacks and a leather pouch the size of a purse. Untying the pouch draw strings, he took out the stub of a pencil, half a candle, a ten-centimetre-long piece of barbed wire with the barbs removed and a box of Swan Vesta matches.

'I'm afraid the matches may be damp,' he allowed, 'but at least they aren't safety matches. I can strike them on any surface if I have to.'

'Why not put them in the tin?' Bob asked.

'Because the phosphorus in them might taint the food,' Ted replied. 'It's poisonous. And, before you ask,' he added with a grin, 'I don't know the German for *I have been poisoned*.'

With the escape kit returned to its hiding place, they went for a spin. The evening was drawing in yet they still had time for a circuit of the camp before the evening *Appell* was called and German guards came round to chivvy them into the barrack for the night.

'How will you get out of the camp?' Bob enquired as they strolled along the path.

'I don't know yet,' Ted confessed. 'Climbing the fence is impossible and cutting through it just as difficult, even if I had a pair of wire-cutters. The guard patrols are pretty regular and a watchtower's never far away. I thought of going out in one of the carts but the guards search them too well.' A shiver ran down his back at the memory of the sentry prodding the sacks with his bayonet. 'My best option is to get away from one of the work parties …'

'When will you go?' Bob asked

'I've not decided yet. But soon. This summer. While the weather's good.'

'You'll say goodbye, won't you?' Bob said.

Ted smiled. 'No,' he replied, 'but you'll know when I'm going.'

Somewhere far off in the camp, the bell summoning them to *Appell* started ringing. They stepped off the path and started to weave their way through an area of prisoners' vegetable plots. Rows of carrots and beetroots were pushing through the soil.

'Of course,' Bob remarked, 'you still lack the most important thing of all.'

'I know,' Ted answered. 'A map.'

It was a warm, still night. Far off in the woods beyond the perimeter fence, a fox coughed. It was a rasping sound, like an old man clearing his throat. Across the pond, a little owl occasionally shrieked. On the end gable of Hut 3, a bulb in a metal bracket cast a circle of dim light on to the bare earth. Every now and then, something flitted through the beam, quicker than the blink of an eyelid.

Bat, Ted thought. Taking insects attracted to the light.

These were the signs he was looking for. If the nocturnal world of animals was busy then it meant that mankind was sleeping.

The sacking that hung over the windows in winter had been removed and the window was ajar to let air circulate. Very slowly, Ted eased the window wider and poked his head out, craning his neck from side to side. Nothing stirred except the bat. He glanced back into the gloom. The tiers of bunks were only just discernible. The only noise that came from behind him was an intermittent snore.

This is not going to be easy, he said to himself. It was a good two-metre drop to the ground and the window was not very large. Furthermore, he had to get out through it in silence. Not only did he not want to alert the guards but he also did not want his fellow prisoners to know what he was doing. It took him at least three minutes to get the lower portion of his body through the window: three minutes during which, at any moment, he expected to hear a guttural German voice. Finally, the sill was level with his chest and he was at the point of no return. He let go of the window frame and dropped to the ground, rolling to break his fall.

Crouching just under the barrack, Ted listened. There was no clatter of curious footsteps on the flooring over his head, no clamour of frantic running feet, no ominous rattle of rifle bolts.

His every nerve as taut as a steel hawser, Ted edged along to the end of the barrack. The sky was clear, with bright starlight broken only here and there by scattered clouds. There was no moon yet the stars gave sufficient light for him to see quite clearly. He paused, gathering not only his courage but also his strength. He was, he thought, like an athlete waiting at the starting line for the sharp report of the starter's gun – although a gun of any sort was the last sound he wished to hear.

Suddenly, there was a hushing noise over his head. Terrified, Ted looked quickly up. The little owl was perched on the end of the barrack roof. It ruffled its feathers, gave a brief screech and stared down at him with its round dark eyes. The fright the bird had given him evaporated. If the owl was not alarmed it meant that it had neither seen Ted nor a sentry.

Encouraged by his apparent invisibility, Ted sprinted at a crouch for the next barrack, slipping into the shadows beneath it. Glancing back, he could see the owl still perching on the roof, watching for the bat swooping under the lamp.

It took him ten minutes to work his way across the camp, moving as stealthily as he could from building to building. With each quick dash, his confidence grew so that, by the time he reached the Parcels Office, he wondered if he was the only person alive in the entire place.

Hunched down in the shadows of a stack of empty

wooden boxes and a few barrels, he surveyed the way ahead. The next piece of ground he had to cover was the most dangerous.

Ahead of him was the main administration building for the camp, its windows black squares against the blackness of the night and the wooden walls. Around the building was a row of the *Kommandant*'s prettifying bushes. Twenty metres to his left, the main gate stood with a light shining down on it from the crossbar of wood above the entrance. Looking at it in the night, it reminded Ted of a grotesque goalmouth backed with barbed wire rather than a net. To one side was the sentry box while, opposite it, was the guardhouse. Another low-wattage bare bulb over the door picked out the steps in vague shadow. Either the sentry box or the building, Ted knew, had to contain a guard.

For ten minutes, he watched the main gate for signs of movement. There were none. At last, he decided to make his move. Tensing up his muscles, he took a deep breath and, hunched up, ran across the dirt roadway. His every step seemed as loud in his ears as an avalanche of pebbles. When he slid into the bushes, the rustle of leaves was as strident as the flames of a vast forest fire.

'*Wer ist da?*' a voice barked out.

Ted peered through the bushes. A guard had stepped out of the sentry box. He had unslung his rifle and was holding it at the ready across his chest.

'*Was ist los?*' another guard called out from the guardhouse.

'*Ich habe etwas gehört.*'

The sentry was looking straight at Ted. He could feel the man's eyes boring into him. At any moment,

Ted was sure he must see him, bring his rifle to his shoulder and take aim.

In the distance, the fox coughed briefly again.

'*Es ist ein Fuchs,*' the voice in the guardhouse replied.

The sentry remained looking straight at Ted. Then he shrugged, slung his rifle back over his shoulder and crossed the gate to enter the guardhouse. The door closed behind him.

Ted, who had not taken a breath since the sentry appeared, filled his lungs with night air. As he did so, he realized with some annoyance that he had trodden in a pile of horse dung left in the road. The stink of it filled his mouth until he could almost taste it and it took him several minutes working with a branch broken off one of the bushes to clean the sole of his boot. It would, he thought detachedly, be ironic if he were caught by smell, not by sight or sound.

Moving along between the line of bushes and the administrative building, Ted reached the end and turned the corner. Here, he was out of view of the main gate and not overlooked by any other building except the German soldiers' mess hut, which he was sure was not used at night.

Standing up, Ted edged along the wall until he came to a window. Running his hand around the casement, he found the hinges and guessed the position of the latch. Removing the length of barbless wire from his pocket, he inserted it between the window and the frame, sliding it upwards. It moved several centimetres before catching on something. Ted wriggled it a little then, with a quick thrust, jerked it upwards. There was a loud click and the window opened.

Placing his hands on the sill, he kicked upwards and swung his head and chest forwards. In less than thirty seconds, he was inside the building, crouching on the floor behind a large desk upon which papers were piled next to a typewriter and a telephone. Against the wall was a filing cabinet and a hat stand bearing a military greatcoat. Ted felt in the pockets in case they contained anything of use to him, but they were empty.

The office, it appeared, was that of a clerk or the *Kommandant*'s secretary. Ted wanted the *Kommandant*'s office.

With infinite care, he pushed down on the handle of the office door. It creaked as it opened. The noise seemed as loud as a tearing sheet of steel. Outside, there was a corridor. Ted moved along it, pausing at each door before going by it. Some were open and he did not want to risk disturbing a sleeping guard. Yet every room was unoccupied.

At the end of the corridor, Ted came to a closed door upon which a hand-painted notice proclaimed *Kommandant*. Praying it was not locked, he eased the handle down. The mechanism clicked and he pushed the door ajar. A glimmer of faint light, provided by the bulb outside the guardhouse, shone through the window.

The office was not as big as he had expected but it was exceedingly tidy. The papers on the desk were stacked in wooden polished trays. A telephone stood, tall and black, in one corner with the cord to the earpiece neatly coiled. Next to it, a silver stand surmounted by a German imperial eagle held two pens and an inkwell. Beneath the window was a bookcase lined with books: beside that was a filing cabinet similar to the one in the first office. On the wall was a framed photograph of Kaiser Wilhelm while on a shelf beneath it was a photograph of the *Kommandant* himself holding a hunting rifle and standing proudly with his foot resting upon a huge wild boar.

What a souvenir! Ted thought. Better than a postcard of the Brandenburg *Rathaus*. Yet he knew he could not steal it. No one could know he had been in the office. Besides, he was not hunting mementoes. He wanted something far more valuable and useful than a petty keepsake.

For a long moment, he stood in the doorway and surveyed the room. He was sure the *Kommandant* would have what he wanted: it was just a matter of knowing where to look for it. Deciding to start with the bookshelf, Ted stepped into the room and, kneeling behind the desk, started to run his fingers along the books as if, by touch, he could divine the contents. It took five minutes to study the contents of the bookcase. A few of the volumes were novels by Charles Dickens and printed in English. One was a German–English dictionary. The rest were in German, the titles and authors' names on the spines printed in ornate Gothic script. None were what he was hoping to find – an atlas. At last, Ted stood up, somewhat disappointed, and turned round.

His heart skipped a beat and his mouth was suddenly dry. His hands started quivering with excitement. Behind the door, fixed by drawing pins to a large noticeboard hanging on the wall, was the very object for which he was looking. It was a large map of Germany.

Admittedly, the map was printed in German but Ted had little difficulty in identifying Berlin. It was more or less in the centre and many lines denoting roads and railways radiated from it like the uneven threads of a spider's web. Working out from the capital, it was only seconds before he located Brandenburg.

'Got it!' he murmured aloud, unable to contain his satisfaction.

A clock on the wall in the corridor outside chimed twice. It was a delicate, silvery ring and, for a moment, reminded Ted of the clock that stood on his grandmother's mantelpiece.

Two hours, he thought. I've another two hours to dawn.

From a drawer in the *Kommandant's* desk, Ted removed a sheaf of plain writing paper. From his pocket, he took out his pencil stub. With infinite care, he started to copy the map, beginning at Brandenburg and moving ever west and north-westward towards the sea.

He was soon engrossed in copying the map as accurately as he could, and to the same scale, marking on the roads and railways, the rivers and canals, noting the towns along the main routes. Yet the more of the map he painstakingly reproduced, the more depressed Ted became. It was a very long way to the sea, even to a point on the nearest coast. It took seven sheets of paper, each running on from the last, to reach the North Sea. And, he thought as he meticulously sketched the last sheet, there were still several hundred miles of ocean to cross before arriving in England.

However, drawing the map had helped focus his mind and, gradually, a plan formed. He would head for the coast then, somehow, acquire a small boat. In this, he would sail down the coastlines of Germany, Holland, Belgium and France to Calais and the English Channel. Once there, he could sail across the Channel to Dover, a distance of not more than thirty miles. At the beginning of the war, he knew Calais had been the main centre for British troops and supplies heading for the battlefields of Belgium. However, there was no way of knowing how the war was going – after all, *Feldwebel* Diepgen had said the Germans were winning – and the port might by now be in enemy hands so, he reasoned, it might be wiser not to land in France.

Ted was so preoccupied with his copying and planning that it was at least five seconds before the sound of a key turning in a lock registered in his mind. The first he knew that he was not alone was when boots started clomping on the floorboards of the corridor. A light was switched on which flooded into the office.

For a split second, Ted froze. The sudden realization that he had left the *Kommandant*'s office door open added to his fear.

The footsteps came nearer. There was nothing Ted could do. The only effective hiding place was under the *Kommandant*'s desk yet he dared not go to it for fear his movement might be heard. Right by the door, the footsteps halted. Ted huddled against the wall beneath the map. The boots moved again and a German soldier entered the office. Looking up from behind the door, Ted could see his every detail, the buttons on his uniform, the curl of his ear, the stubble that had grown on his chin during the long hours of nocturnal sentry duty.

The guard slowly surveyed the office.

'*Ist hier jemand?*' he asked softly.

Ted's heart thumped. Surely, he thought, the German must hear it. It was as loud as a bass drum in his ears.

His survey of the office over, the guard gradually lowered himself to his haunches and peered under the *Kommandant's* desk. He turned his head this way and that to investigate the shadows.

If I had hidden there ... Ted left the rest of the thought unsaid in his head.

Satisfied no one was hiding under the desk, the guard stood up and, muttering under his breath, stepped backwards, closing the door behind him. The footsteps retreated and the outer door opened then closed, the key grating in the lock once more.

For several minutes, Ted kept utterly still. It could be a trap. The guard could still be there. At last, he risked a movement. It drew no hurried steps along the corridor, no raucous voice.

Folding the copies of the map into his pocket, Ted returned to the clerical office. The first light of dawn was just breaking outside, filling the sky with a feeble glow. Checking there were no sentries in sight, he lowered himself to the earth, reaching up to wedge the window shut. He could not refasten the catch and hoped no one would notice it was unlatched.

In the early light, it was impossible for him to return to the barrack so he drew his knees into his chin and huddled behind the bushes, shivering in the chill of the dawn. When the camp was fully awake, with prisoners and guards moving about, he chose his moment and stepped out from behind the bushes and, passing the queue outside the cookhouse, headed for his barrack. Once on his bunk, he prised the knot of wood out and, rolling the maps as tightly as he could, slid them in beside the money. This done, he lay back, elated by his night's achievement.

Like a choir of ghostly souls, the sirens on the watchtowers started to wail mournfully. Prisoners, engaged in a game of cricket on the earth pitch of the parade ground, stopped play. Pankhurst, who was bowling, halted in mid-stride and put the ball in his pocket. The batsman at the far wicket swung his bat up to rest on his shoulder. The wicket keeper stood up. Everyone looked around to see the cause of the alarm.

'What's Fritz up to now?' Bob wondered aloud, glancing towards the perimeter fence where the guards were unslinging their rifles.

His question was soon answered. A platoon of German troops ran in through the main gate.

'It's a hunt,' Pankhurst remarked as he left the cricket pitch to stand next to Ted.

'Tally-ho!' another prisoner remarked sarcastically. 'Anyone laid down aniseed to confound the hounds?'

'They'll not find anything,' Bob prophesied. 'They'll just blunder about, make a mess of things and retreat thinking they've kept us on the hop.'

The search party, under *Feldwebel* Diepgen's command, headed straight for the ablutions block.

'Don't fret yourself,' Wilkie said, appearing at Ted's elbow and reading his thoughts.

'But what about your laboratory?' Ted asked in an undertone.

'Moved,' Wilkie replied enigmatically.

For ten minutes, there was a lot of banging and shouting in the building. Finally the *Feldwebel* and his team appeared, one of them drenched to the skin.

'Some of them taps ain't too secure,' Wilkie commented nonchalantly, looking up at the sky with a look of feigned innocence on his face. 'One little knock and – whoosh! 'S'enough to make you believe in a just God, ain't it?'

After mustering the search party, and dismissing the soaking-wet soldier, the *Feldwebel* marched his squad directly across the parade ground, kicking the cricket stumps out of the ground on the way. Ted broke into a sweat. He was making a beeline for Hut 7. The *Feldwebel* stomped up the steps and, flinging the door back on its hinges, disappeared inside.

'Nothing you can do about it,' Bob murmured, seeing the look of apprehension on Ted's face.

'No,' Ted replied sullenly.

'Don't worry. They'll find nothing,' Bob reassured him.

Yet, in his mind's eye, Ted saw Diepgen take out a pocket knife, prise the knot of wood loose and remove the maps.

For a quarter of an hour, the prisoners listened to a cacophony of thumps and crashes emanating from the building. Eventually, the search party re-appeared, formed up outside and marched back across the parade ground and out of the camp with *Feldwebel* Diepgen at their head.

'There they go, empty-handed,' Bob remarked with the satisfaction of someone who knew he had been right all along.

'Better go and tidy up,' Pankhurst said laconically.

The interior of the barrack was in a state of shambles. Clothing and personal possessions were strewn about. The stack of firewood had been kicked down and half a dozen bunks had been pushed over. Straw from torn palliasses, books and papers littered the floor.

As he crossed the barrack, Ted saw his bunk was one of those that had been toppled. The frame had split, the wood splintered open at just the point where he had hollowed out his hiding place. From two metres away, he could plainly see the cavity. It was empty.

His mouth went dry and, for a moment, he felt weak at the knees and sat on the edge of the next bunk. It had been pulled back from the wall but was still upright. Tears began to gather in his eyes. They were not tears of misery, nor even of rage, but of frustration at his bad fortune, at his sheer stupidity. The Germans never searched under the barracks. If he had put the money – and the map – in the brick pillar, this would not have happened.

Slowly, he began to gather up his clothing from the floor. All his efforts had been in vain. The risk he had taken breaking into the *Kommandant*'s office, the saving of the money and the hoarding of high-energy food were now utterly futile. In his mind's eye, he could see *Feldwebel* Diepgen sitting at his desk in his office in the administration building counting the money and pondering how on earth the maps had been drawn: and who had drawn them.

Any minute now, Ted thought, Diepgen would return accompanied by a squad of armed guards with bayonets fixed, stomping into the barrack, demanding to know who had copied the maps. Ted knew he would have to own up. To keep silent would be to condemn his fellow prisoners to reprisals and he could not expect them to suffer on his account. He would be marched away, put in solitary confinement, probably slapped about a bit and starved for a week or two. After that, escape would be out of the question. In Diepgen's eyes, he would be a marked man for whom the *Feldwebel* would always be on the lookout.

As he bent to pick up a crumpled shirt upon which there was the dusty imprint of a German military boot, Ted spied something white and thin lying under the fallen bunk. It was the tight roll of maps. Immediately, his misery vanished. With a quick and deft movement, he gathered it up and thrust it in his pocket. The money, however, was nowhere to be found.

That evening, as the prisoners sat around the stove talking and playing cards, Ted lay on his palliasse. Being on the top bunk, with no one able to overlook him, he removed the maps from his pocket and smoothed them out.

The scale, which he had copied on to the first sheet, was in kilometres. Very carefully, with a length of string, he started to work out the least distance from Brandenburg to the North Sea coast of Germany, laying the string out along railway lines. Travel by road, he reasoned, would take too long and he could easily get lost. Besides, the longer he was on the run, the more likely he was to be apprehended. Jumping a train seemed the best method of reaching the coast. Certainly, with his money lost, buying a ticket was out of the question. So too, he thought, was buying food. He would have to steal whatever he ate after his own rations ran out.

The nearest point on the coast where he might be able to acquire a boat was, he reckoned, the port of Bremerhaven. Stretching the amount of string used along the scale, he figured it would mean a rail journey of 408 kilometres. Dividing this figure by ten and multiplying the result by six, he arrived at an approximate distance of 244 miles. It was not as great as he had feared but there was a huge risk he had not counted on. From the map, it was clear he would have to change trains at least five times, once in the city of Hannover and once again in Bremen.

As he wound the string round his fingers, this realization somewhat disillusioned him. He had naïvely thought the railway might run directly from Berlin to Bremerhaven by way of Brandenburg and began to wonder how he might tell which train line to follow out of a major city. He would, after all, not be travelling in passenger carriages but in freight cars on goods trains.

As he pondered this seemingly insurmountable problem, his eyes wandered over the map. Suddenly, as if the route was lit up in lights, the answer to his dilemma presented itself.

About forty kilometres north-west of Brandenburg, the River Havel flowed into the River Elbe, which, in turn, wended its way across Germany to the major seaport of Hamburg. Ted unravelled the string again and laid it down along the line of the two rivers.

Hamburg was, he guessed, 298 kilometres from Brandenburg with another 100 or so from the port to the open sea at Cuxhaven. This translated into 239 miles to the North Sea. No changing trains, no getting lost. What was more, he considered, if he could obtain a suitable boat at the start of his journey, there would be no need to steal one on reaching the coast.

The possibility had no sooner entered his head than he knew the very vessel he could use. It was moored alongside the jetty at the farm.

It was drizzling. Before the work party column had marched a hundred metres from the camp gate, Ted's clothes were covered in a fine dew. The wool of his jersey began to smell like a wet dog in a warm room. Around him, the prisoners moved almost sluggardly, as if the weather was an oppressive weight upon their shoulders. Even the guards seemed depressed. Only one person was in good spirits and that was Wilkie. He hummed tunelessly to himself, the rhythms of the music in his head keeping step with his feet.

'Wot you got t'be so merry aboot?' muttered Scotty, a short and muscular Glaswegian bombadier.

Wilkie gave him a nod and a wink and carried on humming.

Walking by Wilkie's side, Ted asked in a quiet voice, so as not to draw a guard's attention, 'Something up your sleeve?'

'What're we plantin'?' Wilkie replied obliquely. 'I'll tell you,' he went on. 'Beet. Sugar beet. Same as yesterday and the day before.'

'And? Have you bred more wrigglers?'

'Show you when we get there,' Wilkie answered.

The column arrived at the farm and the units formed up separately. As Wilkie had predicted, they were given wooden trays of sugar beet seedlings and set out for the farthest field on the farm. It was not until they assembled at the field, and the sentries had taken shelter under a nearby elm tree, that Wilkie addressed the team.

'Right, lads,' he began in his customary way, 'we got beet again. An' I ain't got no idea what caterpillers eat beet. But ...' He paused, glancing towards the guards. They were leaning against the trunk of the elm. One was lighting a small clay pipe. 'I do know what do eat beet.'

He put his hand inside his jersey and carefully withdrew it. Between his fingers poked the head of a sparrow.

Ted was puzzled. Sparrows did eat beet seedlings: they would level them to ground in three pecks. Yet he failed to understand how a pet sparrow could help the prisoners decimate a whole field. For a start, the minute Wilkie opened his hand, it would fly off.

'How did you catch it?' Scotty enquired.

Wilkie opened his hand. The sparrow made no attempt to fly off.

'I didn't,' he said. 'I made it.'

From even close up, the sparrow looked exactly like a real one. Its eyes were bright beads, its feathers were the correct shade of mottled brown, its beak was short and pointed and its legs stick-thin.

'Papier mâché,' Wilkie continued, 'painted over with varnish to stop it meltin' in mis'rable weather like we got today.'

'I don't see 'ow a wee toy birdy ...' Ginge began.

'Oh! 'e won't do no scoffin',' Wilkie interrupted, 'but 'is chums will. In my shirt, I've got six more just like this one. We stick 'em down close-ish to each other in the middle of the field. When we've gone, you can bet your last silver tanner the wild sparrers'll flock in to join what they think're their real mates at a banquet of beet. Now,' he added, 'I can't ben' down to plant if I got a shirt full of dummy chirpers. So –' he started handing the birds out – 'one each. When we get to the middle of the field, I'll make a loud cough. You let your sparrer go. Put 'im near a plant so's it looks like 'e's 'avin' a good munch. That should do the trick.'

By one o'clock, the fake sparrows had been deployed and the prisoners returned to the farm for their midday break where, to keep out of the drizzle, they were permitted to stay in the barn. The usual black bread, cheese and *sauerkraut* were issued along with some apples. Ted ate his bread and apple but saved the piece of hard cheese, wrapping it in his handkerchief and slipping it into his pocket.

When they had eaten, most of the prisoners sat

about or lay on the bales of straw stored at the back of the barn. Ted positioned himself on a barrel at the barn door from which he had a panoramic view of the farmyard. To his left across the wide cobbled yard was the farmhouse. A large wagon was parked up against the wall. The German guards, with one exception, were in the farmhouse kitchen. Ted could hear them talking and occasionally laughing. The only guard not with the others sat hunched up in the driver's seat of the wagon, the drizzle dripping off the peak of his helmet. As there was no other way in or out of the building, the one sentry was sufficient to watch the prisoners.

Next to the farmhouse was a stable, the doors open. A pile of steaming hay and horse dung, recently cleared out of the loose boxes, stood on the cobbles. Fifty metres beyond the stable were the old mill building and the river. To the right of the barn was a large, empty pigsty, on the other side of which was a small orchard of fruit trees surrounded by a post and rail fence that led down to the mill.

Studying the lie of the land, Ted reckoned his main difficulty were the first ten metres of cobbled yard. If he could get behind the pigsty it would be easy for him to reach the mill unseen.

'Give you a pfennig for 'em,' Wilkie said, joining Ted at the barn door and sitting next to him on the barrel.

'For what?' Ted replied.

'Your thoughts,' Wilkie explained. 'Can't give you a penny. Ain't got one.' He followed Ted's gaze across the farmyard, guessing what he was thinking. 'Wan' a bit of a diversion?'

'Yes,' Ted answered.

''Ow long?' Wilkie asked.

'Twenty seconds.'

Wilkie winked, went into the barn and reappeared with Ginge and another prisoner. They walked across to the guard at the wagon and started to talk to him. Ted watched. Wilkie leaned up and offered the German a cigarette. As soon as his hand started to go down to the packet, Ted slipped off the barrel and headed for the pigsty.

He reached the corner of the low wall and slid behind it. No alarm was raised. Crouching down, he went along the rear wall of the sty until he reached a gate in the orchard fence. Passing through it and, keeping low and to the far side of the orchard from the farmyard, he circled round towards the mill.

On reaching it, Ted slipped behind a holly bush growing against the rear wall of the mill. A window in the wall was broken. He peered through it. The mill was clearly no longer used. A derelict cart stood in the centre of the building. Beneath the window were stacked old seed boxes and a pile of rotting flour sacks. Some wooden buckets, one of them containing a rusting grain scoop, lay on their sides by the double door and various lengths of rope were loosely coiled here and there. On the floor to one side of the window was a pile of bat droppings testifying that no humans regularly visited the place.

Working his way along the wall, Ted reached the river. There, before him, still tied to the jetty, was the boat.

He had to get a close look at the vessel but he could not just walk out on to the jetty. To do so would put him in full view of the farmhouse and the guard on the wagon. Even crawling out on to the jetty was a risk for there was nothing on it behind which he might hide. There was, he realized, no alternative but to wade out to it.

Quickly undressing, Ted slipped into the water. It was cold and snatched at his breath while his feet sank into an oozing slime of mud and underwater weed. Undaunted, he waded under the jetty, coming up between it and the side of the boat. Careful not to put more than his head in view over the gunwale, he lifted himself up. The boat tipped slightly to one side under his weight. Quickly, he glanced into the vessel.

It was obvious it had not been used for some while. There were three or four centimetres of rainwater collected in the bottom, the oars were stowed away, the rowlocks were rusty and the bow, pointing away from the bank, was besmirched with grey streaks where a water bird of some sort had perched. The rigging, however, was intact and, although there was no foresail, there was a main sail lashed to a boom. Ted tested the knots in the mooring lines. They were loose, suggesting they had not been recently tied. That the vessel was seaworthy seemed beyond doubt.

Suddenly, footsteps slapped on the planking of the jetty. Ted let go of the side of the boat, filled his lungs with air and allowed himself to sink, making as little of a splash as possible. Peering up through the water, he saw the vague shadow of someone outlined against the drizzling sky move along the jetty towards the end. Every time they crossed over a crack between the planking they blocked the light out.

For nearly a minute, he held his breath. They did not return to the shore but stayed at the head of the jetty. At last, he had to surface. As silently as he could, he took a breath and started to move towards the end of the jetty, all the time studying the daylight coming through the gaps between the planks. When he reached the end, there was no one standing there.

He was about to admit to himself that he had imagined the whole thing when there was a sudden squirt of white liquid into the river not fifty centimetres from his face. Ted started back in the water, banging his head painfully on one of the jetty posts. In response, there was what sounded like a slapping of wet towels. The hull of the boat bobbed violently in the water and a large grey goose clumsily took to the air from its perch on the bow.

Gaining his composure and rubbing a growing bump on his head, Ted waded back to the bank, clambered out of the river and hurriedly dressed behind the mill. He used one of the rotting sacks as a towel to dry as much of himself as he could. In a few minutes, he had retraced his steps to the farmyard where the prisoners were leaving the barn to form ranks for their return to the fields. He slipped into the gathering unseen and set off for another five hours of sugar beet planting.

'Got somethin' cookin'?' Wilkie enquired as they turned out of the farmyard.

Ted made no reply. Instead, he mimicked Wilkie's nod and wink.

Wilkie grinned in response and said, 'That's m'boy!'

As they approached the beet field, a flock of at least

a hundred sparrows rose from the centre to fly off in the direction of the railway line, twittering with alarm and annoyance.

PART FIVE

LATE JULY AND EARLY AUGUST
1917

A warm afternoon sun shone through the window of the carpentry shop, picking up motes of sawdust hanging in the air like pollen. At the end bench, Dan Copley was planing what would be the base of a marquetry chessboard. The rhythm of the plane on the wood was even and measured, the shavings curling up from the blade.

Ted stood back and gazed at the *Evelyn* resting on a makeshift stand on the carpentry bench. There was still work to do to her but it was little more than fitting out. The hull was finished, the main mast was in place, the decks completed and the hatches fitted.

He had even finished the rowing boat, although he had yet to varnish it. He was most proud of that. Ten centimetres long, it was an exact replica of the one he and his father used to row out to the boat in Clovelly harbour, or ashore on Lundy Island when they went there to check their crab pots or collect puffins' eggs.

'She looks grand,' Bob said approvingly. 'I could never make something that good.'

'Yes,' Ted agreed immodestly, 'she does, doesn't she.'

'Do you think she'll float?'

'There's only one way to find out,' Ted replied.

With Ted carrying her, they took the *Evelyn* through the camp towards the pond, setting her down on the sand at the water's edge. A number of prisoners who were swimming came out of the water to admire the boat and watch her launched on her maiden voyage.

'Of course,' Ted commented as he waded into the water up to his shins, 'she'll need sails before she can really prove herself. They might make her top-heavy.'

He lowered the vessel gently into the water, holding his hands under her hull to steady her, then, gradually, let go. She took up her own buoyancy and floated free. The waterline came to within a centimetre of where Ted had projected it would. The vessel seemed stable. Ted flicked the top of the mast with his finger. She listed to port then quickly settled back on an even keel.

Satisfied at the *Evelyn*'s apparent balance, Ted slightly angled her rudder, turned her with her prow facing out into the pond and gave her a gentle push. She sailed out into the pond, her bow cutting through the tiny wavelets on the surface, her stern leaving a ruffled wake behind her.

As she turned to starboard to head back to the bank, accelerating slightly in the breeze coming off the pond, Ted could imagine her much bigger, with his father standing at the wheel, and his grandfather preparing nets on the foredeck with his old baccy pipe clenched in his teeth. He could see himself, standing at the bow, watching for the dolphins that swam alongside every summer in Bideford Bay. He could almost hear their clicking, squeaking conversation.

Gradually and smoothly, the *Evelyn* turned in an arc to return to the shore where she ran aground.

'Perfect!' Bob exclaimed.

Ted did not bend down to pick the model up. He just stared at it for a long moment then said quietly, 'She's yours, Bob. A real souvenir of Brandenburg.'

'I couldn't accept ...' Bob began, then he fell silent. Suddenly, he realized what this offer meant.

Ted picked the *Evelyn* out of the water, brushed the damp sand off her hull and held her out.

'Consider it a loan, then,' he said.

'I'll finish her off,' Bob promised. 'Set her rigging, sew her a set of sails. Get another coat of linseed oil rubbed into her deck.'

They carried the *Evelyn* back to the carpentry shop, dried off the hull with cotton waste and removed the mast so she could fit into the cupboard. Closing the door, they set off for a spin.

'When are you going?' Bob asked when they were out of earshot of both other prisoners and the guards patrolling the wire.

'Soon,' Ted replied enigmatically.

'Have you got a plan?'

Ted smiled to himself and said, 'Yes, I've got a plan. A damn good plan at that.' Yet he did not elaborate upon it and Bob did not ask.

'And your supplies?'

'All ready,' Ted answered, 'and, before you ask, yes – I've got a map.'

Bob was incredulous.

'A map!'

'Five kilometres to the centimetre. About eight miles to the inch. Not too detailed but good enough.'

'How did you get it?'

Ted grinned, tapped his nose and said nothing.

After the evening meal was over, the prisoners took it in turns at a large bucket at the door of Hut 7 to wash their cutlery and tin plates. Ted hung back, waiting until Pankhurst was busy rinsing off his fork and spoon before approaching him.

'George,' he said tentatively.

'Yes,' Pankhurst replied, drying his utensils on a square of cloth.

'I'm ...' Now that he was face to face with him, Ted was at a loss as to how to tell Pankhurst what was on his mind. 'I want to say goodbye.'

'Yes,' Pankhurst said. 'I thought you might one day. When are you going?'

'Tomorrow,' Ted admitted. 'I've told no one else.'

'Don't,' Pankhurst advised. 'No one will blab to Fritz but they might just let a careless word slip in earshot of a guard.' He stood up and put his cutlery in his pocket. 'Do you have everything you need?'

'I think so,' Ted answered. 'I've been hoarding food.'

'Indeed you have,' Pankhurst rejoined, 'and hiding it under the hut in one of the pillars.'

Ted stared at Pankhurst and said, 'How did you know?'

Pankhurst laughed. 'I might not presently be in charge of a mess-deck, but I'm still a Leading Hand,' he reminded Ted. 'I know all the tricks. I've seen young lads like you aboard ship hiding letters from your lady-friends and I've seen old sailors stashing away their baccy and rum ration. There isn't a nook or cranny in one of His Majesty's destroyers I don't know about. Do you know once, in Alexandria, I saw an Engine Room Artificer hide a two-foot-long crocodile in a bilge compartment.' He grew serious. 'Have you got it all worked out?'

'As best I can,' Ted replied. He looked around to make sure no one could hear him. 'I've found a boat,' he explained succinctly. 'I'm going down the river to the sea. Then I'm going to sail south along the coast of Germany and the Low Countries until I get to France.'

'That's a long journey,' Pankhurst remarked. 'And a dangerous one. Are you prepared to fail?'

Until now, Ted had been so confident that he had not considered the possibility he might not make it. Suddenly, he realized his chances were slim in the extreme. He had to travel by river through Germany then along the enemy coastline for at least 350 miles until he reached the English Channel.

The obstacles started to mount up in his head: the boat moored at the farm might not be suitable for the open sea and he would have to somehow find another; he would need fresh water and food, which would mean landing in enemy territory; he would have to brave summer squalls in the North Sea.

After a long pause, Ted said soberly, 'I think so.'

'Remember this,' Pankhurst continued, 'a man can live for days, even weeks, without eating yet he cannot last two days without drinking. Once you reach the sea, be sure you have sufficient fresh water. Never go out of sight of land. And –' he put his hand on Ted's shoulder – 'take care, Ted.'

For the remainder of the evening, Pankhurst sat by himself at the end of the table by the stove. Although it was summer, the stove was kept lit in order to brew tea. Just before the Germans switched off the electricity for the night, he came across to Ted who was lying on his bunk.

'Will you do something for me, Ted?' he asked.

Ted turned on to his side and raised himself up on his elbow. Pankhurst held out a sheet of paper folded twice into a square.

'Can you see my sweetheart gets this?' Pankhurst went on. 'Her name's Louise. Louise Hawkins. I call her Lou. She lives at the village stores in Flimwell. That's a little village in Sussex. You don't need to go there. I've put the address on it. Post it when you get back to Blighty. I just want ...' he paused for a moment '... just want to tell her I love her without *Hauptmann* Vogel reading it first.'

Ted reached down and, without speaking, took the letter.

That night, Ted could not sleep. He lay quite still on his back, staring at the rafters of the barrack roof. It was 298 kilometres to Hamburg. That was 180 miles, more or less. Then another fifty miles to the sea. If, he reasoned, the current in the river flowed at five miles an hour, which speed he did not consider unreasonable, then he could reach the city in less than two days. If he had the wind behind him, he might even make the open sea in less time.

'I'll fix it,' Wilkie assured Ted as they marched towards the farm with the early sunlight warm on their backs.

'A minute's sufficient,' Ted said.

'One minute, ten minutes. It don't make no difference,' Wilkie replied. 'We can fool Fritz for ever.' He gave a glance at Ted's waist. 'You got the entire Navy stores tucked in there?'

Ted smiled and said, 'Not quite.' Then, a little concerned, he added, 'Do they show?'

Wilkie shook his head. 'No, you look thin as a pencil, chum.'

Ted was relieved. His entire escape kit was in the two small hessian sacks under his shirt, suspended from his neck on a length of twine just long enough to allow each sack to hang above his belt and under his arms.

'When we get to the farm, stick close to me,' Wilkie ordered. 'I'll give yer the signal. Take yer time.'

At the farm, the guards reported to the farmer. Wilkie gave the nod to half a dozen prisoners from his barrack and they started to mingle round the entrance to the barn. Under cover of them, Ted slipped into the building, went to the very back, quickly unbuttoned his shirt, pulled the hanging cord over his head, tugged the sacks out and buried them deep in the hay up against the rear wall.

'All set?' Wilkie asked as Ted reappeared, doing up the last of his shirt buttons.

'All set,' Ted confirmed.

Wilkie gave him a little friendly punch on his arm and murmured, 'Yer on yer way.'

The beet seedlings having all been planted, and duly ravaged by sparrows, the prisoners were ordered to return to the cabbage fields to till between the rows, weeding and turning the soil beneath the cabbages. The crop was patchy. While there was a fair number of healthy plants, there were wide areas where the crop was stunted and weak.

'Don't dig too close to the cabbages,' Wilkie said as they started down the parallel lines of cabbages. 'The wrigglers wot survived will 'ave turned into chrissy-lisses by now. They'll be snug in the leaves. Don't want to disturb 'em. When they 'atch, the butterflies'll be straight on to the leaves, layin' a new lot of eggs. The cabbage white,' he added authoritatively, 'can 'ave two generations in one year. So wot the spring wrigglers don't munch, the summer ones do.'

The day dragged on. Ted found it hard to concentrate. His mind was a mingling kaleidoscope of worries, fears and apprehensions. At the midday break, he surreptitiously checked behind the hay. Everything was safe and untouched which keyed his spirits up. However, when the day's work at last came to an end, Ted had serious misgivings.

'Knots in yer belly?' Wilkie asked as they left the fields.

'Steel hawsers,' Ted answered.

'I was like that, night before me weddin',' Wilkie confided. '"Shall I, shan't I, shall I?" Shilly-shallyin' about like a tomcat on a tightrope, I was. Nex' day, plain sailin'. Mind, she walked out on me six weeks down the road.

Ran off with a fishmonger from Billin'sgate. Mark my words, sonny-Jim. Doin' a bunk from Fritzland's goin' to be a doddle compared to a married month with Mavis Scrutton. I bet,' he added thoughtfully, 'she 'ad that fishmonger filleted inside a fortnight.'

The prisoners entered the farmyard and lined up in front of the barn. Wilkie signalled to Ted to join the line at the back. The guard with the limp started to count the prisoners off. As soon as he had passed Ted by, Wilkie smiled and whispered, 'We'll double up when they count off back at the camp. Now, scarper! Give me love to dear ol' Blighty.'

Ted took three paces backwards into the barn, slid behind the door, ran quickly round the walls and dived behind the hay. The prisoners marched off and silence fell, broken only by the clucking of hens scratching about in the farmyard.

For the remainder of the evening, although the farmer and his family went to and fro about the farmyard, no one entered the barn. Later, someone rode up on a horse. When the twilight was almost turned to darkness, Ted collected up his escape supplies and crept from the barn. The farmhouse door was open, casting a weak oblong of light from an oil lantern across the cobbles. From within, Ted could hear people talking. The visitor's horse, tethered to a post, snuffled in an oat bag suspended from a hook on the farmhouse wall.

Following his earlier route, Ted went behind the pigsty and through the orchard. Several sheep, grazing under the fruit trees, shuffled away from him, looking like shaggy rugs on legs.

At the mill, Ted did not bother to keep to the rear

but went straight on to the jetty. He balanced his two small sacks of supplies on the seat in the stern of the boat so they did not touch the rainwater collected in the bottom. This done, he returned to the mill where, after a few moments groping about in the dark and pricking himself on the holly bush, he found the two wooden buckets he had seen. Taking these and the grain scoop, in addition to a few lengths of rope, he returned to the jetty.

Making sure the oars and rowlocks were still aboard, he gingerly stepped into the little craft and cast off the mooring ropes. With one of the oars, he thrust himself firmly out into the river. For a moment, the craft seemed to head straight for the opposite bank but then, gradually, she slowed and turned, her prow facing downstream as the current caught her.

For fifteen minutes, using the grain scoop, Ted baled out the rainwater. He was afraid that, as he baled, more water might appear but it did not. The boat might have been unused but her hull was sound. This task done, and feeling much reassured, Ted lowered one of the buckets over the side, rinsed it out and refilled it with water. This was to be his drinking supply.

Half an hour before midnight, a new moon rose. By its light, Ted studied the first page of his map. From the lie of the land, the course of the river and a railway bridge he had passed under, he estimated he had already travelled about twelve miles. Just as dawn was breaking, the river turned back on itself. After another five miles, the Havel reached its confluence with the River Elbe. As Ted steered the boat into the middle of the wide river, it accelerated sharply. He had, he thought, about 200 miles to go to the open sea.

Around mid-morning, Ted reached the town of Wittenberge, where the river was crossed by a road and railway bridge. Approaching the first, he saw with dismay it was lined with policemen and soldiers. At least a dozen rifles were resting on the parapet. And everyone was looking upstream – in his direction.

There was nothing Ted could do but continue sailing straight for them. To veer off into the right bank would have meant landing near the town, while crossing to the left bank would have looked distinctly suspicious. With the hair on the nape of his neck prickling, he made for the central arch of the bridge.

Suddenly, from behind the bridge, a small steam launch appeared with four policemen in it. It turned into the main current, the bow breaking waves as it headed for Ted. With no alternative but to face them off, he sat bolt upright at the rudder, reasoning it was best to appear obvious and open.

The current bore him on, nearer and nearer. At fifty metres, he saw two of the policemen in the boat had their pistols drawn. Another, standing in the bow, started waving frantically at him and shouting incoherently. Ted, not understanding a single word, waved back. This prompted one of those brandishing a pistol to gesticulate wildly with his weapon.

'*Zur Seite! Aus dem Weg!*' the policeman in the bow yelled, flapping his hand sideways.

Frantically, Ted tried to summon up his knowledge of German. He knew what he wanted to say. He had mentally prepared for this moment. Yet he just could not find the words.

'*Aus dem Weg!*' the policeman hollered again. '*Schnell! Schnell!*'

The policeman levelled his pistol straight at Ted. The threat brought his mind immediately alive.

'*Ich bin ein Fischer!*' he shouted back, holding up one of the hessian sacks in the hope it might look like a fisherman's bag.

Then it dawned on him what the policeman was demanding. *Aus dem Weg* meant *Get out of the way*. Ted swung the tiller hard over and the boat listed sharply. He corrected the angle, turning to face down river once more but, out of the main stream, slowed to a snail's pace. No sooner had he regained his original course than a cacophony of small arms fire erupted over his head.

Ted flinched instinctively, ducking down and screwing his eyes tight. At any moment, he thought, he would feel the red-hot pain of a bullet cutting through his flesh and he wondered, in a strangely abstract way, what it would be like to die.

However, not a bullet struck the boat. After what seemed like minutes, yet which was in fact little more than twenty seconds, Ted opened his eyes. He was passing underneath the bridge. He could see the soldiers and police firing into the river a hundred metres upstream. Tiny splashes exploded where the fusillade was hitting the surface.

As soon as the shooting had started, it stopped. The

last reports echoed off the buildings. The police boat came sharp about and the man in the bow threw a line with a grappling hook attached to it into the river. Two others helped him pull it in. Impaled on the prongs Ted could see the limp body of a man.

For the next two hours, as the boat continued down-river, Ted kept seeing the vision of the man's body float across his mind. He wondered who he had been: a criminal, a deserter from the army – or an escaped prisoner of war.

By now, he considered, the alarm must have been raised back at Brandenburg. *Feldwebel* Diepgen would already be investigating. It would be only a matter of time before the boat was found missing.

Later in the afternoon, Ted sailed beneath the next river crossing point, a bridge near a village called Dömitz. Now on the fold between the third and fourth sheets of his map, he estimated he had travelled about halfway from Brandenburg to the open sea. However, the current was perceptibly slowing and, as he negotiated two sharp meanders just past the bridge, he pondered on what he might do to pick up speed. Raising the sail was the most obvious answer yet there was insufficient wind to fill it.

As a clock in a nearby village chimed six, the river straightened. Ted felt suddenly very tired. His back ached from sitting for so long in the stern of the boat, his arms ached from controlling the rudder to keep the little craft in the current and his legs were stiff. He realized he had been on the river for the better part of twenty hours and exhaustion was rapidly overtaking him. His eyes grew heavy and he found it difficult to concentrate.

A mile into the straight, the right bank gave on to open farmland criss-crossed by ditches. There was not so much as a low hedge against which to hide. On the left bank, however, dense woodland came right down to the water's edge, willows leaning over to trail their leaves in the water. Ted gently nudged the tiller over. The boat headed under one of the willows and the hanging branches caught on the mast to form a camouflaging curtain.

Tying the bow of the boat up to one of the exposed roots of the tree, Ted opened one of the sacks and ate first some of the cheese then a block of chocolate with a ship's biscuit soaked in jam. The chocolate made him thirsty so, using the grain scoop as a mug, he took a drink of water from the bucket then clambered ashore. After testing the knot in the mooring rope, he lay on his back upon a litter of dry leaves and closed his eyes. Within ninety seconds, he was fast asleep.

It was, Ted guessed, well after midnight when he awoke, shivering. The moon had already risen, bathing the countryside in a grey light. A cold wind was blowing through the draping fronds of the willow. Even in the shelter of the tree, small wavelets lapped at the bank. The boat had swung round on her mooring rope so that her bow pointed up-river.

Still not quite fully conscious, Ted sat up, rubbing his arms to restore his circulation and stop his teeth from chattering. Listening to the wind hissing through the branches, it was several minutes before he realized the direction from which it was blowing. It was an easterly.

Hastily, he climbed into the boat, casting off the rope and pushing against the bank with his foot. The craft resolutely refused to move. A pang of fear ran through him. If the vessel had run against a root of the tree, it might now be impaled upon it, the hull holed. In his mind, he heard Pankhurst's lesson. *With a ship, it's not that simple,* Pankhurst's voice said. *With a ship, you have to tether both nose and tail.*

'Damn!' Ted swore aloud.

Yet his feet were dry. The boat had not filled with water. She could not be holed. He glanced up. In turning in the wind, the mast head had become entangled in the branches of the tree.

Ted knotted the mooring rope to the root once more, returned to the bank and started to climb the tree. He was conscious that he dare not fall. If he were to slip, he could break a bone on the bank: if he fell in the water, he would be soaked and, in the cold wind, would soon start to lose his body temperature. By dawn, he thought, he could be chilled through and dying of exposure.

With extreme care, he edged out along a thick bough. It bent under his weight. Reaching the tangle of branches holding the mast fast, he began snapping them with his bare hands. The mast was almost free when the bough splintered. Ted slid down it, head first, his fingers scrabbling for a hold. The bough swung into the bank and hit the trunk of the tree. The impact dislodged him. He fell heavily to the ground, badly grazing his knuckles. Winded, he lay gasping for breath and cursing his stupidity.

Bruised, but with no bones broken, he cast off a second time. The boat slid out from its hiding place into the full glare of the moonlight, the wind quickly taking it downstream.

With cold fingers, Ted fumbled with the ropes tying the sail to the boom. He managed to free the canvas then, kneeling so as not to unsteady the boat, he raised the sail. It was not large and the canvas, which had obviously been folded for a long time, was stiff and crackled audibly as it unfurled. Even in the moonlight, Ted could see patches of mould growing on it. Yet the condition of the material was irrelevant. The wind filled it, the seams and stitching held and the boat quickly picked up speed. The bow slapped through the waves, blowing an occasional fine spray into the air.

At dawn, Ted passed a town. From his map, he reckoned it could be Lauenberg. He was cold and shivering once more, his clothing damp from the spray.

At this moment, he thought, Bob and Pankhurst would be stoking up the stove in Hut 7. Wilkie would be in the cookhouse, lining up to collect the rations for his barrack. The air would be filled with warm steam and the cloying aroma of boiling porridge.

'Boiled eggs, with soldiers of bread and butter, and toast with orange marmalade,' someone whispered over his shoulder.

'Bob!' Ted exclaimed.

He turned. There was no one there, just the wake of the boat and the banks of the Elbe slipping by in the early light.

'I'm daydreaming,' he said aloud.

No sooner had he spoken than Ted realized this was

dangerous. His mind was wandering, hallucinating. He was so exhausted it was affecting his brain.

'Concentrate!' he ordered himself.

Several miles beyond Lauenberg, the river began to curve south. Passing an island, Ted lowered the sail. It meant his journey would slow somewhat but he was loath to waste his energy tacking to and fro. It would be quicker to rely upon the currents. Besides, studying his map, he discovered he had made very good time and was, he calculated, less than twenty miles from Hamburg.

After a long loop south, the river turned north-west and Ted hoisted the sail once more. The wind remained brisk but it was a clear morning promising a fine summer's day.

A few miles from Hamburg, the river branched into two. Ted, believing it was best to keep as far from the city as possible, steered for the southerly channel. Other vessels began to appear, moored to the shores or riding at anchor in mid-stream. Most were barges loaded with timber and coal. Some carried their cargo secure under tarpaulins. From a few, smoke eked out of little chimneys protruding from the stern, quickly dissipating in the wind. Ted could imagine the bargees snug in their bunks and a fleeting vision of his mess on HMS *Nomad* flashed before his eyes.

Coming up rapidly on two barges moored side by side, Ted noticed a line of laundry hanging from a thin rope tied between two stanchions projecting over the side. The barges, overloaded and riding low in the water, put the laundry within easy reach. Ted eased the tiller over and sped close by the steel hull of one.

As he passed, he raised his arm as high as he could. His fingers snagged on a seaman's jersey. This, in turn became tangled in the next item of washing. The wooden clothes pegs popped free as each item was wrenched from the washing line. In less than five seconds, Ted acquired two thick woollen jerseys, a pair of trousers, a shirt, three vests and one long woollen sock.

'That's today's trip to the shops done,' Ted murmured to himself, grinning at his good fortune. Yet his theft had a serious purpose. He knew he had insufficient clothing should the weather turn against him once he was out at sea. Now that shortcoming was rectified.

On either side of the river, there were quays with steamships lying alongside. Ted dropped the sail and relied upon the current once more. It was, he considered, better to move slowly through the dockland. This would not arouse suspicion, it would enable him to manoeuvre around any vessels that might get in his way and it afforded him a good view of the shipping.

Taking out his pencil stub and turning over the first sheet of his map, which he no longer needed, he started scribbling down the basic details of every ship he saw. This, he knew, would be useful military intelligence when he finally reached England.

As the sun rose, its warmth began to seep into Ted's skin. It also dried his clothes out although he did put on one of the jerseys for the wind still had an edge to it.

It was well over an hour before Ted was clear of

Hamburg and heading for the open sea. The river was now much wider and the currents fickle so he hoisted the sail. By mid-afternoon, the banks of the river were over half a mile apart and little more than thin lines on the horizon. The wind became blustery and the spray now tasted of salt. Ted was forever changing course to keep the sail filled and ducking to avoid the swinging boom hitting the side of his head.

The sun was low in the sky when Ted spied the town of Cuxhaven off to port. This, he knew, was the point of no return. From here, he was in the open sea and beyond the range of his map. All he had to do now was to head for the town, keep the coast in sight and follow it until he reached France.

His plan, he decided, was to sail during the day then land at night, hiding up where he could, replenishing his fresh water supply and, with luck, finding some form of food. How long it would take him to reach France he had no idea and he did not really care. He was no longer a prisoner of war and he would, within a few days, be out of German waters.

Steering a course for Cuxhaven, Ted was elated. Once round the headland upon which the town was built, he would be truly on his way. He began to hum to himself, breaking into song.

'It's a long way to Tipperary, it's a long way to go,' he sang. 'It's a long way to Tipperary, to the land that I love so ...'

The wind snatched the words from his mouth the moment he had uttered them.

He was about 400 metres from the shore and headed on a course straight for the beach when, quite suddenly, there was an ominous crack, as loud as someone snapping their fingers. Halfway up, a split appeared in the mast. The wind gusted again. As Ted watched, there was a creaking squeal and the top of the mast broke away, dragging the sail down and over the side.

'No!' Ted yelled in despair.

The moment the canvas hit the water, it became waterlogged. Its weight caused the boat to heel over alarmingly. The sea lapped at the gunwale. The boat started shipping water. In next to no time, she would capsize.

There was nothing for it. Ted frantically worked at the knots in the rigging. It took him long minutes to separate the sail from the remains of the mast, during which time more water washed inboard. His stolen clothing was soaked through.

At last, the sail was free and floated off. His next task was to bale out the boat. This took another ten minutes. By the time he was finished the boat had drifted at least 700 metres from shore. Without a sail, Ted had no alternative but to try and row towards land in the hope he might run the boat up on the beach. He unshipped the oars and set to.

For a quarter of an hour, he rowed hard. His efforts were in vain. The tide was running and the wind, blowing with it, was driving him helplessly out to sea. Tired, disconsolate and frightened, Ted stopped rowing as the coastline of Germany faded in the distance.

When darkness fell, the wind dropped and the sea calmed to a low swell. Ted hunched himself into the stern of the boat and tried hard not to think negatively about his predicament. Yet the more he tried, the more the hopelessness of his plight played upon his mind. He attempted to think of something positive and kept a lookout for any passing ship.

He was, he reminded himself, in the sea lanes for entry into one of Germany's busiest ports: on the other hand, there was a war on. No ships would show running lights. He would be hard pressed to see one unless it came straight at him. Then, it occurred to him, it might ram and sink him.

An hour after dark, Ted spotted lights on the horizon. It was difficult to tell how far away they were but, undeterred, he started shouting in the hope they were a vessel. Yet they did not move and it was then he remembered that six miles off Cuxhaven were several of the Frisian Islands. This realization depressed him further for he could tell he was drifting past them, out into the vast expanse of the North Sea.

Although he fought to stay awake, Ted could not help dozing off only to come round a few minutes later in a near panic. He was growing cold again as well and had no dry clothing. What was worse, his sacks of provisions were sopping wet. The two remaining ship's biscuits were sodden and the lumps of sugar which he had been counting on as a source of energy had dissolved. The remains of the cheese were softened and crumbling.

His greater worry, however, was his water supply. When the boat had tipped, at least half his fresh water had been spilt. He was now down to less than a few centimetres in the bottom of the bucket and even this tasted slightly salty from the spray. Pankhurst's warning kept running through his mind, repeating itself over and over: a man can live for weeks without food but only days without water.

Thinking of Pankhurst, Ted reached inside his shirt where he had tucked the love letter with the maps and his list of shipping details. The envelope was limp and damp. Just touching it brought on a terrible sadness. He would never see Pankhurst again, never deliver the words that would give his sweetheart hope. He would never see England again, or Clovelly, never walk down the steep cobbled streets of the village to his parents' home. He would never again step aboard the *Evelyn* for a day's fishing with his father off Lundy Island.

A week from now, he thought, I'll be nothing but a corpse floating in an open boat, food for gulls. Or worse, he considered, floating on the surface of the sea, ghost-white and bloated like a dead seal, being nibbled at by fishes or ripped to shreds by sharks.

The thought of sharks prompted other memories. He recalled Saturday night talk in the snug bar of the Red Lion, the pub by Clovelly harbour wall. Old sailors with faded tattoos and battered caps had wetted their whiskers with four-ale and regaled their fellow drinkers with tales of giant squid as long as a ship, narwhals with unicorn horns which could pierce a boat, whales that could swallow a cutter whole, crew and all.

When Ted had questioned the veracity of whales eating men and boats, the old men had lowered their glasses with a slow deliberation. The Holy Bible, they had said with a solemn patience born out of many a questioning unbeliever. Had not Jonah, they reminded him, been thrown overboard by his shipmates and swallowed by a huge fish? Had he not spent three days and three nights in the belly of that great fish before being fortuitously cast upon the land?

Ted grew edgy. Those old men had sailed the seven seas, braved the storms of Cape Horn, the cannibals of the Pacific and the pygmies of the East Indies who cut your head off and shrank it to the size of an apple. Shuddering with cold and fright, he thought at least some of their stories could be true.

The night dragged on. Clouds drifted across the panoply of the Milky Way, blotting the stars out for a few minutes at a time. Ted imagined an invisible ogre drawing his hand across the sky. When the moon rose, its light was periodically extinguished, plunging the sea into a temporary darkness that seemed to be blacker than death itself.

In these interludes of darkness, Ted's imagination started to run riot. A sudden breaking wave made his skin crawl and he fancied he could see a slimy wet tentacle slipping silently over the edge of the boat, a slug of enormous proportions slithering over the planks of the hull. It slid silently towards him, rising up to grip him by the throat, the suckers latching on to him, drawing his blood and breath away.

Then the moon would come out and he would see it for what it was, the end of the mooring rope and the soggy, stolen sock. When the swell raised the little craft up on a crest, he believed he could see the hump back of a whale at the bottom of the trough between the waves.

At last, partly from exhaustion and partly in order to try and drive these morbid and terrifying thoughts from his mind, Ted curled up in the bottom of the boat, pulled some of the damp clothing over himself and fell into a troubled sleep.

What woke him, he could not say. One minute he was fast asleep, the next he was fully awake. He listened intently. He was sure he could hear a deep, rhythmical throbbing. Seeming to come from below the hull of the boat, it was like a heart thumping far down in the ocean.

Holding on to the remains of the mast, Ted stood up and surveyed the sea. The moon was much lower in the sky, its light shimmering across the gently rolling swell. The wind had died completely, the boat more or less wallowing stationary.

'Ridiculous,' he said aloud, as if the sound of his own voice was enough to drive away his fear. 'I'm just hearing things.'

Yet there it was again. Under his feet. The regular thump-thump of a massive heart driving hot blood round the arteries of a grotesque monster.

Something caught his attention. Fifty metres from the boat, an eye on the end of a stalk was looking at him. Its pupil glistened in the moonlight.

'Get away!' Ted yelled impotently.

Unblinking, like the eye of a prehistoric reptile, it turned this way and that. With his free hand, Ted waved at it in the vain hope that this might somehow scare it off.

Then, as he stared at it, the sea began to boil and rise. Spray rose vertically from its surface. The throbbing grew louder until it filled Ted's head. From the centre of the boiling water, a black monster rose into the night, its snout piercing the air and snorting like a bull about to charge. Then the moon slid behind a cloud.

Ted screamed yet no sound would come from his mouth. He clutched on to the broken mast with both hands, screwing his eyes tight shut so he might not see death take him. The boat rocked as the boiling water spread out from the beast and engulfed it.

All was suddenly silent. The throbbing ceased. The sea began to settle and the boat stopped tossing from side to side. Ted opened his eyes. It must be, he thought, an hallucination. Any minute now, he would wake up under the willow branches, back in his bunk in Hut 7, back in the mess on HMS *Nomad*, back in his own room overlooking Clovelly harbour and the noise of the monster would be nothing more than the tide running up on the shingle of the shore.

Yet the monster was still there, silent and black and foreboding, waiting its moment.

'Get away from me!' Ted shouted, his voice taut with fright.

The monster answered with a metallic clinking like the dolphins had made in Bideford Bay. Yet they had been friendly.

'Get away from me!' Ted repeated.

The moon came out from behind a cloud.

Riding on the sea, not twenty metres away, was a submarine. A figure on the deck briefly shone a small, bright torch on Ted. Its beam blinded him and he put his hands over his eyes.

It was all over. Ted knew he had no choice. He had either to surrender or die a lingering and horrible death from thirst in an open boat. Crestfallen, he called out, '*Ich bin* …' It occurred to him he need not speak

143

German. 'I am Ted Foley, a British prisoner of war escaped from Brandenburg Camp.'

'And I,' came the reply, 'am Sub-Lieutenant Young of His Majesty's Submarine *Seasprite*.'

SUMMER 1919

The locomotive pulled slowly up to the buffers, the smoke from its funnel collecting under the roof of the station before the sea breeze whisked it away. The pistons sighed and hissed as the steam valves were opened to release the pressure.

'Portsmouth Harbour! Portsmouth Harbour!' a porter shouted as he walked along the platform. 'End of the line! Change here for the Isle of Wight ferry.'

The carriage doors began to open. Holidaymakers and day trippers from London appeared. Some carried suitcases, other picnic baskets. Children, eager to get to the beach, carried buckets and spades. They were followed by sailors carrying cylindrical canvas kit bags over their shoulders or officers with leather valises and polished briefcases.

Everyone made their way to the platform barrier, passed the ticket collector and stepped out on to The Hard, the street running along the waterfront beside the station. There, they divided into three groups. Holidaymakers headed back on themselves for the paddle steamer bound across the Solent for Ryde or went to the right for the omnibuses to the beach and pleasure gardens at Southsea. The sailors set off along The Hard to the left, making for the main gate of the Royal Naval Dockyard.

Ted waited until most of the passengers had departed before he stepped down from the train. The station was built on a jetty. He could see the water beneath through the cracks between the planks of the platform. It gave him an uneasy feeling. He could not help being reminded of a much smaller jetty near a farmyard in the heart of Germany. The only difference was that, now, he was on top of the planks, not holding his breath in a metre of water beneath them.

His kit bag was heavy and unwieldy. Being new, with his name starkly stencilled in black upon it, the canvas was rough and rubbed against his neck. His new boots, polished so highly that they caught the sunlight coming through the sooty glass panels in the station roof, were a bit tight and one of them creaked with each step.

He reached the platform barrier, presented his travel warrant to the ticket collector, went down the steps and turned left along The Hard. It was lined on one side with pubs and officers' uniform tailors, chandlers' stores and little shops selling the kind of merchandise sailors might need just before embarking upon a long voyage – needles and thread, tobacco and matches, boot brushes and combs, spare silks and lanyards. Across from the buildings was the mouth of Portsmouth Harbour with the town of Gosport on the opposite shore.

Ted made his way along the row of shops and taverns, avoiding sailors and merchants, carters delivering barrels of beer, urchins selling small tins of boot polish and laces and an elderly woman dressed in a voluminous shawl handing out moral tracts to anyone who would take a copy.

As Ted reached her, she thrust one into his hand, saying, 'Young innocent! Beware the enticements of Satan! Succumb not to the vices of a godless world! Beware the temptations of the flesh and fall not into the realms of sin but rise up into the Glory of the Lord.'

'Thank you,' Ted said, somewhat embarrassed.

Ahead stood the archway of the main dockyard gate. A line of sailors queued at the guardhouse to enter. Ted joined the queue, gratefully swinging his kit bag off his shoulder to stand on the cobbles by his side.

Full circle, he thought to himself.

Since he had last entered through this gate, he had served on HMS *Nomad*, been sunk in the greatest sea battle of the war, held captive by the enemy, escaped and been rescued. He had also spent a while in a military hospital and a longer time back at Clovelly, resting and recuperating, building up his muscles, which had wasted during his imprisonment and helping his father land the sardine catch.

But now, he was back. No longer a mere ship's boy, he was a naval rating. He looked down at himself. His bell-bottomed trousers were neatly pressed with the requisite number of horizontal creases and his lanyard was pristine.

A hand touched his arm. He turned to find a young woman standing next to him. Slim and pretty, about his height, she was wearing an ankle-length skirt and a long-sleeved blouse with lace frills at the collar and cuffs. Upon her head was a navy-blue straw hat, perched at a slightly jaunty angle.

'Hello, Ted,' the young woman greeted him, her violet eyes looking into his, a faint smile playing on her mouth.

'H-hello,' Ted stammered, taken aback that she should know his name.

'I'm Lou,' she said. 'Lou Hawkins. Or rather, I was.' She held up her hand to display a plain gold wedding ring.

Leaning forward, she kissed him on his cheek. Her lips were soft and slightly damp. Looking over her shoulder, Ted saw George Pankhurst standing a little way off by his own kit bag. He was dressed in the uniform of a Petty Officer.

'Come and have a drink with us,' Lou invited Ted, putting her arm in his. 'George says there's plenty of time.'

'Hello, Ted,' Pankhurst greeted him. 'I see we're to be shipmates again.' He ran his eye up and down Ted's uniform. 'My, lad! You look every inch one of His Majesty's jack tars.'

'Doesn't he just!' Lou said. 'Any day now, you'll be sweeping young ladies off their feet.'

'Girls can't resist a matelot's uniform,' George added. 'Now, let's have a swift half pint of ale before we go back to sea.'

Arm in arm, with Lou in the middle, the three of them walked towards the nearest pub. As they passed the old woman with the moral tracts, she gave Ted a scowl so black and accusing that, for a brief moment, it almost – but not quite – scared him.

GLOSSARY

Appell (German)	roll-call
bargee	a crew-man on a barge
Blighty	military slang for England
bo'sun	a boatswain
bo'sun's pipe	a small silver whistle used by a bo'sun to give signals to the crew, to ceremonially pipe an officer aboard a ship and to call hands to action stations: it is the naval equivalent of the bugle in the army
bulkhead	a wall between compartments in a ship
calibre	the size of a gun measured by the interior diameter of the barrel
censor	a man whose job it was to read prisoners' letters home to ensure no information of use to the enemy was being mailed; he also had to check

	incoming parcels and letters
Chief Petty Officer	(CPO) the most senior rank below that of a commissioned officer
chippy	a ship's carpenter
chronometer	a very accurate clock or watch
clipper	a very fast, streamlined sailing ship
clump	a concrete or stone anchor for a buoy
companionway	a narrow, steep ladder between decks
cutter	a large rowing boat usually crewed by at least six oarsmen
ditty box	a small, lockable wooden box in which an ordinary sailor kept his sewing kit, razor and other personal possessions
Feldwebel (German)	Sergeant-major (army rank)
fender	a cylinder of rope or canvas-covered cork used to stop a vessel rubbing against another vessel or a dock
fitting out	furnishing a new ship with her final equipment
flotilla	a small fleet of ships, usually vessels of destroyer and frigate size (or smaller)
fo'c'sle	the pointed deck above a ship's bow (shortened from forecastle)
Hauptmann (German)	Captain (army rank)

hessian	the coarse cloth used for making sacking
hawser	a thick rope used for tying up ships alongside quays
jack tar	an ordinary seaman (naval slang)
lanyard	a short cord, part of a sailor's uniform
Leading Hand	the senior-most sailor on a mess-deck
lighter	a barge or similar craft
to list	to lean to one side
Lt Cmdr	Lieutenant Commander (abbreviation)
matelot	an ordinary seaman (naval slang; from the French for a sailor)
mess/mess-deck	a sailor's living quarters
palliasse	a thin, straw-filled mattress
Petty Officer	(PO) the next rank down from a Chief Petty Officer
pfennig (German)	a low denomination coin
pinnace	a small launch
pom-pom	a small calibre, multi-barrelled quick-firing gun
Pompey	naval slang for Portsmouth
port/port side	left; the left-hand side of a ship
PoW	prisoner of war
QF gun	a quick-firing gun of medium-size calibre
rathaus (German)	town or city hall
rating	an ordinary seaman (sailor) in

	the Royal Navy
Rittmeister (German)	Captain of horse (army rank)
scrambled egg	naval slang for gold braid on an officer's cap
silk	the small black bandanna-like scarf worn by naval ratings
skiff	a small fishing boat
stanchion	an upright support for a guard rail, rather like a steel post
starboard	right; the right-hand side of a ship
tanner	a six-penny coin, also known as a sixpence
tiller	the bar that controls the rudder in a small craft
wardroom	the officers' mess on a ship
Wipers	British Army slang (in the Great War) for the town of Ypres, in Belgium

Historical note: the remains of the seaplane that flew from HMS *Engadine* in the Battle of Jutland may been seen in the Fleet Air Arm Museum at Yeovilton, in Somerset.